To Niamh,
Happy read
Love Phoebe
Alexandra

CW00868021

ALIGHT

ALEXANDRA HART
AND
PHOEBE SLEEMAN

CRANTHORPE
—MILLNER—
PUBLISHERS

First published by Cranthorpe Millner Publishers (2022)

ISBN 978-1-80378-035-1 (Paperback)

www.cranthorpemillner.com

Cranthorpe Millner Publishers

To every twelve-year-old who has ever had a dream. Work hard at it.

PROLOGUE

I was watching her that night.

I wasn't peeking through the window; I didn't have cameras on her; I certainly wasn't staring into a crystal ball. But I was watching her. It doesn't matter if you don't believe me. Not to be rude, but this isn't about you.

The voices grew louder downstairs and she flopped dramatically onto the bed, feet raised skyward like a toppled china doll. She was like that, you see.

Earlier that day, she had stood outside the house and let defiant tears leave the twisted taste of salt upon her tongue. The car had driven off, and her sister hadn't looked back. Emilie, being as dramatic as she was, would have felt more secure with a large argument and last minute reconciliation. But everything seemed too normal. Not important enough to make her cry.

And besides, Lizzie was only going away on a long holiday with her friends and would be back in a month or so. She was far too sensible for scenes of arguments and reconciliations like Emilie wanted anyway.

1

Yet an all-encompassing sense of emptiness spiralled inside Emilie's bowel, something I can quite sympathise with myself. Perhaps she was angry she hadn't been included in her sister's adventure, instead being confined to the mundanity of home.

Such mundanity wasn't to last long, of course, but as yet she was unaware of what awaited her.

"We have something to tell you," her parents had said that night as they sat down on either side of her on the sofa.

"Emilie..." her father started, then looked over her head to his wife, wavering. His eyes pleaded with her to be the one to break the news. Emilie squirmed uncomfortably on the sofa, feeling trapped between the unsaid words as much as between her parents on either side.

"We feel that this summer is the right time for you to spend a while at your great aunt's house," her mother finally declared. She laid a hand on her daughter's leg, firm but caring. "Your *biological* great aunt."

That inescapable word twirled itself around Emilie's mind: not quite excited, not quite fearful. It wasn't uttered aloud particularly often, especially not by her mother. Emilie held her breath, suspended in a mix of emotions she couldn't untangle.

Emilie truly loved her parents, and she knew they didn't care she wasn't actually their own, even if her sister Lizzie was. Her father had always said that family was love, not genetics. She never knew her biological parents. She jokingly liked to claim: "I'm sure they must have been angels for me to be as I am!", though secretly she wished they had provided her with slightly better genes. Of course, at night, she invented outlandish tales of famous celebrities sweeping their long-lost daughter away to a bedazzled week in Paris, with stylish fashions and bubbled sweetness and fur-lined affection. However, no fantasy could replace her real parents; real love given by real enough people for her.

Emilie still hadn't decided quite which emotion she was feeling when her father spoke once more. "Your great aunt has wanted to meet you for quite a while now," he added, slightly too enthusiastically, or perhaps apologetically. "She lives with her grandson, who is about your age, and she can introduce you to your -" he stopped, swallowing what he was about to say.

"My what?" Emilie's eyes and ears perked up. There were many questions running through her mind, but the mysterious pause couldn't help but catch her imagination. I inwardly cursed her father's mistake. He should have known better.

"Your... family history, somewhat," he finished, a glimpse of relief at finding the right words passing over him before he looked away.

Emilie slumped back – history was not exactly something that thrilled her, and family history seemed especially tedious.

Why had her aunt suddenly reached out now? Where did she live? How long was she to go for? Why had her parents never mentioned a great aunt before? Nowhere in her parents' carefully cautious answers could Emilie see the thrill of a story.

But that just about decided it for her. A great aunt, family history, a sister who had left her, parents who were shipping her off. Her potential for excitement fizzled out as I saw anger haze her eyes. Biological families were all very well and good for imagining adventures, but useless when you were forced into visiting their elderly members. I saw her pupils narrow, a "how dare you" forming upon her tongue as she squared up to her parents.

And so, as much as she loved them, all she felt at that moment was a melodramatic wish that she had been adopted by some other people; people who didn't just send her away to some old relative she had never met before. If Emilie had perhaps been a little older, a little wiser, she would have been able to see that anger was her defence against the hurt. But for now, anger alone seemed justified to her.

Relishing in her righteousness, Emilie stood up, exclaiming, "As if Lizzie leaving wasn't enough!" and ran to her room, slamming the door with a flourish. She is, to this day, the only person I know who can pull that off.

Familiar with their daughter's tendency to think the worst and act accordingly, Emilie's parents exchanged a shared grimace as the slam of the door made the plastic chandelier swing alarmingly above their heads.

"I knew it was the wrong decision," Emilie's father sighed, freeing himself from his wife's eye contact and staring at the floor instead. Faint sobs from upstairs echoed into his disappointment. I don't know whether his wife noticed the slight hint of venom I detected in his words; he was rather defensive when it came to Emilie's feelings. He hated even the slightest reminder that their daughter had brought 'complications' with her.

"Well, I'm not too keen on it either," replied Emilie's mother. She wasn't flinching at Emilie's tearful reverberations like her husband, but concerns about the future still seemed to somersault across her mind.

It was at this point in the proceedings that Emilie flopped dramatically onto her bed, while downstairs her failed acceptance of the news led to a full-scale argument. Or rather an 'intense discussion' as Emilie's father told her later when he came to kiss her goodnight.

"Please, darling, we haven't really got a choice," he pleaded with her. "Besides, it's only fair your biological family gets a chance to discover how incredible you are too!" he joked, leaning over to kiss her on the nose. Despite the tears, Emilie giggled, and then tried to turn it into a failed cough. "It won't be for long," her father continued. "After all, it will only seem empty here while Lizzie's away."

Shrugging her shoulders and wishing him goodnight, Emilie settled down again. From the unfurling of her lips, it appeared that her anger was evaporating, but I wouldn't quite call it a truce. Emilie wondered if her mother would also come up, but remembered she never visited after a reconciliation well solved. A nice breakfast would be waiting for her the morning after instead.

And so, after her father's footsteps stopped thudding down the stairs, Emilie rolled over to stare at the fluorescent stars stuck on the ceiling. When she was younger, she used to wish on them every night. And the warmth of wishes past, held in their yellowy plastic, finally softened her resolve.

She decided, and I swear I could see the moment the thought filled her eyes, that it wouldn't be so disastrously bad going to her great aunt's for a few weeks. Lizzie's understated departure and her parents' sudden news overwhelmed her again for a second, but she rolled over to her side and held back the tears, lest they wash away her (albeit fewer) more rational thoughts.

I pitied her in that instant. She seemed to have a continuous battle between logic and melodrama that fought to control her actions. And I know my fair share about jousts of the mind. She had already touched me, and people don't often do that. It was a shame she couldn't see me.

I have changed my mind about what I said at the start. It matters what you think of her, it matters that you believe me. I think you'll learn to care for her.

I really do.

PART ONE
ETTY'S MANOR

CHAPTER ONE

Emilie

My imaginings in the great aunt department were something along the lines of a frail old lady in a musty old house with whom I would constantly be having tea or keeping up small talk about the cost of shawls. But as we turned away from yet another little village and began to work our way up a long drive, I knew I had underestimated her.

The drive led up to a mansion that looked to be as old as the earth it was built on. I could see in my dad's face that he hadn't been expecting it either, although he pulled on the same sturdy look as ever. The hope of adventure began to stir in me.

The house itself had battlements crowning the tips of the roof and strange little extensions poking out in all directions, as if they had been an afterthought. It looked like it couldn't quite make up its mind which era it was from. If Lizzie had been with me, I knew I would have received a detailed description of all the types of 'architectural influences' that were cramped into this single building. *That was certainly one thing I didn't miss.*

Our car pulled up in front of three stone steps that led to grand oak-faced double doors. My dad pulled me in for a hug across the front seats, holding on a fraction too long. I got out, feeling a flicker of excited nausea pulse through me. I climbed to stand upon the highest stone step in front of the doors. Glancing over my shoulder, I saw Dad nod to me, with a look that told me he would wait until I was safely inside before he left. And yet, despite his reassurance, I stared at the mammoth doors without moving. *Just knock, Emilie*, I told myself, but for some reason I couldn't.

What had been excited nausea now moved closer to dread. Thoughts whirled through my mind of what might await me. Had my parents even met my great aunt before? I was pretty sure I'd read a story one time where a girl was taken to a crumbling manor, locked in, and left all alone. It had a happy ending, but who knew what could happen to me. Perhaps I'd never see my family again. It took all I had not to turn and run back to Dad, reminding myself that an adventure was what I'd always longed for. I must have waited for a whole minute – just standing there, willing myself to knock. But before I could find the full resolve, the doors swung open with a screeching moan of rust-ridden hinges, leaving me staring up at the two oddest people I have ever seen in my life.

One: the oldest lady imaginable (picture your grandma in your head and then quadruple how old she looks). Wisps of cloud-fluff white stuck out straight from her head, and her eyes, even from their deep position beneath the wrinkles, pierced a clear blue. But that wasn't the most surprising thing about her. Most surprising was the fact that she was not frail or stooped, she was not in a wheelchair, nor did she have a stick – in fact it had been her who had pushed open the heavy double doors.

Two: a boy unlike anyone you've ever seen before. He wore an extremely odd collection of clothes – shirts over tops under ties through jumpers – that would have looked simply ridiculous on anyone else, yet somehow he pulled it off. His ink black hair, the same colour as his eyes, dropped across his forehead messily, but his chin was defined enough to give him all the confidence he needed.

And as I took in their appearances, the peculiar pair seemed to be scanning me in a similar sort of way. The old lady's eyes stared into mine, forcing my gaze downwards. And yet, for her oddities, there was something about her, something that drew me to her. She didn't look like she would lock me in her manor house and leave me all alone – but I wasn't quite sure.

She broke the silence: "Come in, we haven't got all

day, you have been standing on that doorstep far too long. I am your Great Aunt Etty and you are late."

She had the authoritative tone of someone who wasn't usually disobeyed, and so, temporarily stunned, I circled and waved to Dad; in return he blew a kiss, the stoic look still spread wide across his face, and he trundled off down the long drive. Summoning my bravery, I stepped inside. The double doors drew shut with a chilling clatter, leaving me trapped in a dimly lit hallway.

***

Azariah

I could tell that Emilie was confused. And I could tell that her father was too, far more than he'd ever admit to her. I waited for the heavy doors to slam and then decided that I'd watched enough for one day.

Anyway, I hope now we've established you do indeed care about Emilie, I think I'll let you know a little bit more about her. After all, it's hard to care very deeply for someone you don't really know.

I suppose I'll start with her appearance, since that's what most people start with, although I'm afraid it might be a bit disappointing. Unfortunately for her wild imagination, at first glance she isn't particularly memorable. She isn't tall and she isn't short, neither is she fat nor thin. Her nose isn't especially big or small and turns up just a little at the tip. Her hair is an ordinary mid-way between blonde and brown, just stretching past her shoulders with a couple of waves, being neither satisfyingly straight nor adorably curly. There are shadows of freckles sprinkled across her nose and cheeks, which blossom in summer like daisies. But then, as Emilie would put it, daisies aren't exactly glamorous. Her eyes are also a somewhat murky brown. That is, unless you look closer. If you do, and only if she lets you, you might see some clear little streaks of blue or green defiantly placed amongst the swampy planes.

Overall, I suppose she is what one might call 'cute', a perfectly good adjective for anyone wishing to compliment her, but certainly not the 'strikingly beautiful' her imagination would like her to be.

Still, her imagination sets her apart. It is a thing of infinite beauty. Its only flaw is that Emilie often lets it put her down. You see, if you can't imagine the perfect situation, it's much easier to be happy with your current one. Whereas, when you are always dreaming up swash-buckling, time-bending, earth-shattering adventures, you tend to feel disappointed when nothing of the sort ever happens to you. That's why Emilie tends to like exaggeration, to transform the mundane into the pretence of adventure.

I hoped it might prepare her for what was coming.

Emilie

"You must be starving."

I jolted; it was the first time I had heard the boy speak. I had been too engrossed in the large dark marble hall we had entered to notice that my great aunt had already disappeared. *So much for small talk about the cost of shawls, she'd barely greeted me!*

"I for one am always veritably ravenous after a long journey", the boy continued, "I always have to take some sustenance with me or I simply perish!" I didn't know what to say but that apparently didn't matter, as the boy started off down the hallway, ploughing on regardless of my unresponsiveness. I had to scurry along quite fast to keep up with him. "We are second cousins by the way; my name is Alphaeus but that's a bit of a mouthful so everyone calls me Alphie. I am five foot exactly and scared of geese and spiders, I'm half-Philipino, I have an IQ of 140, and my parents are dead."

I thought maybe I should say something to this but he didn't pause long enough for me to arrange my thoughts.

"I have been simply dying to see you. It can get quite lonesome up here; I mean, there are the twins in the village of course, I'll introduce you to them when we next go down, but often in the middle of winter we have whopping great storms and get snowed in with absolutely no living being in convenient dist~~a~~

He broke up his speech by repeatedly blo~~v~~ a piece of ruler-straight hair from his eyes.

"Nobody can get up here when it snow~~s, we are~~ completely estranged from civilization. No food, no post, no milk. But don't fret; we have an emergency supply cupboard of tinned food. And you'll always know when it's dinner time around here whether it's snowing or not because we have an excessively loud gong to declare it. It's immense fun for the first day or so but after a while that noise begins to creep its way into your dreams in the most confusing of places."

We had been walking down the same endless hallway throughout his entire speech, I could already feel myself wanting to adventure down the corridors on either side and through the potential hidden passageways. Perhaps I'd stop a band of smugglers who had hoped to get their loot out under a cover of snow. I stole glances into dust-cloaked rooms through cracks in doors and wondered what secrets might lie under the years of clutter, but we were walking at such a pace that it was hard to take everything in.

We stopped abruptly at the end of the corridor, turned left, and entered into a low roofed kitchen which had a warmth of gentle light about it. It was cosy and inviting, quite unlike the rest of the house we'd passed, and I liked it immediately. I had never seen or imagined a kitchen like it (I mean, kitchens aren't that fun to imagine) but somehow it felt familiar. Felt homely. My _reat aunt was already seated on a stately oaken chair when we entered, at the head of a square-set table. *How did she manage to get there so quickly?*

"Sit down, child," my great aunt commanded. Her tone was kind and airy but her voice itself as strong as thunder. Obediently, I perched on the edge of the nearest stool to the doorway. It was nothing like the one my aunt sat on opposite me.

"Alphie, go get Emilie some bread and milk."

Alphie did as he was told, setting the meal in front of me with a smile. It wasn't until I saw it that I realised how hungry I was. The bread was warm, freshly baked, delicious. I wolfed it down.

My great aunt allowed me some time to eat while she sipped on a cup of tea. Never once did she take her piercing eyes off me. I made sure to stick out my pinkie when I picked up my milk, she seemed to have that sort of effect. But the first sip was so cold it practically gave me a brain freeze. I winced and placed it back down with a small shake of my head.

My aunt gave Alphie a look, and I straightened my back to make up for my impolite behaviour. I sipped again from the milk, as if to prove I could do it maturely, but it didn't seem half as cold the second time. In fact, I might have even described it as pleasantly warm.

Confusion flickered through me and I glanced back at my aunt. There was something I couldn't read in her expression. It wasn't a judgemental look she gave me, it wasn't even a thoughtful one. I felt like I had lost my ability to understand the human face.

I finished my milk and placed the glass quietly back on the table. "Would you care for some water too?" Aunt Etty asked. I nodded, and Alphie leapt up to fetch me some. I watched in amusement as he rustled through the endless parade of cupboards, slamming each door open in turn. I could see mismatching china in every crevice possible - funny little teapots with more handles than a teapot should own, forks with at least eight prongs each.

Every cupboard was searched through until Alphie reached the end of the counter. "I'm afraid we might be depleted of fresh glasses, Grandma," he sighed, his voice echoing through the china as he pulled his head out of the cabinet.

"Oh, do stop worrying, Alphaeus," came the slow response. "I have already fixed the issue". I turned back to see that my empty milk glass had been filled with water. She must have moved silently to fill it up, though obviously clumsily as little droplets dotted on the table all around the glass too, giving it a rained-on appearance. It confused me that I hadn't noticed her do it, and the look of pained disappointment on Alphie's face, so dramatic compared to the fact all he'd failed to do was get me some water, almost made me want to laugh.

But before I could begin to question much more, Aunt Etty had turned to question me. "Now, tell me, child, what do you know of your parents?"

I froze mid-thought. This struck me as a strange first question to ask. No 'how was the traffic on the journey' or anything. I had no choice but to answer it, so I told her truthfully all that I knew. That I had been abandoned on the steps of an orphanage by my birth mother who had disappeared without saying a word, adopted by my parents when I was two, and had grown up with them for the last decade. Nobody had come to claim me, and nobody had heard of what happened to my mother after she left me on the doorstep. Of course, I didn't say it quite like that. I couldn't resist a few little exaggerations here and there, but I told it as truthfully as I could because I didn't think my aunt would quite appreciate the daring tale of my childhood that I told to most people. I also had the feeling that she knew a lot about me already.

"I see," she said when I was finished. She looked interested, at least I think she did. Sometimes I can tell that adults don't believe my stories; they get this horrid look in their eye that tells me I'm a foolish little girl and that they see right through me. Aunt Etty didn't seem convinced by my elaborations either, but neither did she seem disappointed. I'm not sure I've ever had that reaction before.

"Thank you, my child."

Aunt Etty continued to ask me a series of seemingly disjointed questions after that. I almost felt like I was being quizzed, but in a gentle way, and I tried to answer as best as I could.

"And now, I believe that it is high time you got to bed. Alphie will show you to your room. There is one place I do not want you to go, and that is the top floor. Remember that. Goodnight."

Reaching her conclusion quite suddenly, she handed me a lantern and ushered Alphie and me out of the room. Yes – a lantern. I loved it, and the forbidden top floor thrilled me even more. I felt like a real storybook character embarking on a new adventure.

I thought her welcome was a bit blunt, but still wouldn't exactly condemn it as cold. She just somehow radiated authority. I mean, when you're that old and still so strong, you simply must. Alphie confirmed this as soon as we were out of earshot.

"You really mustn't mind Grandmother, she can be a bit astringent and forbidding, but once you know her and she knows you she is ineffable in her kindness. Your bedroom is on the third floor, opposite mine..."

He carried on talking as we walked back down the corridor, leaving me no time to ask what 'astringent' meant, and took the second flight of stairs we had passed. Unlike the first, which welcomed visitors with a sweeping first step and beautiful old railings, these were much smaller. Their stony dullness froze my feet even through my shoes, and I glanced down in envy at Alphie's huge, crimson slippers.

The stairs were pretty steep, and I was embarrassingly breathless by the time we reached the top. We followed a passageway full of judgemental portraits, each displaying the same piercing blue eyes as my great aunt. It felt as if they were sizing me up, deciding whether I, as their descendant, was worthy of their blood. At the end of the passageway was an enormous tapestry of a knight on horseback. I was held by a few seconds of confusion before Alphie lifted the tapestry and opened a door behind it. It was a curiously tiny door with little decoration. We ducked through and came into a short, round, carpeted landing with three doors surrounding it. Alphie opened the one on the left and bowed, quite ridiculously, saying, "Your room, m'lady." Laughing, I curtseyed back to him and entered through the door. I guessed that my stay at Aunt Etty's would be rather amusing with Alphie around.

"My room is opposite. And that over there -" he pointed to the third door, "is where you may refresh yourself. You must be desperate to after your interminable journey here." And with that, he closed the door, leaving me alone.

The room was curved around the circular landing, making me realise that we were, in actual fact, in the tower which I had spotted from the driveway. Ahead of me rested a bay window, with the curtains already drawn against the darkness outside. I could just about make out a large bed pushed awkwardly against the wall next to me, not quite fitting with its unusual curve. The sight of it was too tempting, and I gratefully collapsed onto the mattress.

But my brain was too excited to sleep. The contrast

of my expectations from the night before with the reality that I had been met with stirred my imagination. I knew it would be fruitless to try to rest.

I lay awake awhile, staring at the ceiling and missing my glowing stars, until I was convinced that Alphie would most probably be asleep. It wasn't that I didn't trust him, even after the little time we'd spent together I could tell that he was worth trusting. I guess it was more that he confused me a little, I was unsure of how he'd react to my wish for a night-time adventure. I slowly crept out of my room and onto the circular landing. The landing was gently lit and so it wasn't until I exited from behind the tapestry that the apprehension began to grow. The house felt different without a lantern, it tingled with invisible life. The dim corridor of ancestors threw disapproving shadows against the walls. It wasn't until the end of the hallway that the realised I didn't actually know my way around. I was met with a collection of corridors and staircases, none of which seemed to go up to that mysteriously forbidden top floor.

I decided to take the corridor to my left, as I was pretty sure the staircase to my right led back down towards the kitchen. I darted across the head of the staircase and into the corridor, but as I did the sound of a whistled tune began and footsteps sounded from down below.

My great aunt.

A shot of adrenaline leapt through me. I felt sure that if she was to find me, she would know exactly what I was searching for, and I felt even more sure that I would be in big trouble. I didn't know which way she would be coming and as I surveyed the corridor I had just chosen, I realised in dismay that it was a dead end – more of a large room than a corridor, and no tapestry marked the end of the room in the hope of a secret door.

Instead, I pressed myself against the wall to the left of the doorframe and yelped as my back came into contact with something hard. I ignored the pain, pushing back in the hope that I wouldn't cast a silhouette and she had not heard my yelp. I could now hear that the whistling had reached the top of the stairs and it was with a sigh of relief that I heard her continue along another passageway.

My heart was too busy thumping for me to continue. I raced back towards my room, barely remembering the way, desperate for the safety of my closed door. The adventure would have to wait for another night.

I made it through the tapestry door relieved, quietly enough not to wake Alphie, and tumbled into bed.

Just before my eyes closed, they rested on a painting of a man and a woman on the wall opposite me. My tired brain could only tell me that they looked young and happy, being far too exhausted to think up anything else more imaginative about them.

And so, with their gaze watching me, I gave in to my dreams.

CHAPTER TWO

Azariah

J decided to check in on her the following morning, and she would have been disappointed to discover that she didn't exactly look like Sleeping Beauty. Her mouth was slightly ajar, her hair was strewn in tangles across her face, and half her leg dangled listlessly out of the sheets. When her eyes flickered open, she stared at the ceiling until she registered where she was. Then, having dramatically jolted upright and swung her legs over the edge of the bed, she smiled as she spied a pair of fluffy slippers awaiting her, identical to Alphie's but in sky blue, her favourite colour.

Jamming her feet into the slippers, she rushed to the window and yanked the curtains open. And once her eyes had adjusted to the brightness, the view did not let her down.

Even though Emilie had sensed that she was near the sea the previous day, the drive leading up to the front of the house blocked it from view. And so, it was in enchanted amazement that Emilie stared at the scene outside her window now. Although the sea was calm at that time of the morning, I know from experience that you can often hear the waves troubling the cliff from inside the house, their rhythms underpinning the events of the manor.

A perfectly manicured rose garden, hidden under a thousand distracting sprinkles of colour, lay under Emilie's window. It was neighboured by a deceptively empty field, which might even be described as bland in contrast, if it weren't for the subtle haze which blanketed it. It was precariously balanced right on the edge of a cliff, so close it looked like it might topple off the edge, taking half of the rose garden with it. In fact, the whole estate was precariously placed on the crumbling rock. And if you didn't know what I know, you'd have been worried it might all soon collapse into the sea below.

***

Emilie

I left the window, feeling like I was in a majestic tale, a fair and noble picture of a damsel in distress through the window from afar. In fact, I'd felt like a princess the

whole night long, laid out on the enormous mattress.
I wandered over to the portrait of the happy couple and let my gaze drift over their faces once again.

The eyes of the painted portrait stared back in an unnervingly realistic way, a way that isn't normally possible to create with paint. No matter how closely I examined them, reminding myself that they were only colour on canvas, they still seemed surprisingly... present. Cautiously, I lifted my finger up to their faces, gently touching each of their eyes in turn. I shivered and pulled sharply away from the frame.

I distracted myself by looking around the rest of the room. The rosebud wallpaper was fading in areas, but the colours still showed through, as if the flowers were merely covered by a winter frost which clouded their brightness. The furniture seemed to have been haphazardly placed around the room: a table by the bed, a mahogany dresser, and a chest, looking particularly dark and mysterious. I tiptoed across to it, excited (yes – I made sure to tiptoe). All of the novels I had read about rotting maps or hidden treasures or ancient loot flashed across my memory. I was sure it would be locked, but, to my surprise, it wasn't. Heartbeat contracting my throat, I lifted the lid to the creak of neglected hinges and peeked inside.

I immediately felt foolish. It looked to be a toy box of some kind. Lizzie would have taken no time to say, "I told you so" if she had been there, smirking, although not unkindly, at my mistake. Disappointed, I gently took out the contents one by one, still hoping that maybe, just maybe, there would be something worthwhile hidden at the bottom. A dusty rosebud tea set matching the wallpaper; a picture book called *The Owl and the Pussycat*; a beautifully carved peg doll; a teddy bear with one arm; a miniature doll's house. When I had emptied all of the contents, a spider scuttled out, probably disturbed by the mess I had made. I returned each of the contents to the chest with great care, trying to make it seem as unbothered as possible. This room must have once belonged to a little girl. *How boring.*

Just as I closed the lid, I heard a knock on the door. A shock of jet hair popped around the side and suddenly Alphie's smile had distracted me.

"Morning!" he beamed, sauntering into my room. His cheer immediately repaired what was left of my foolish feelings. "First, I'm going to give you a simply smashing tour of this place, there are so many wonderful nooks and crannies to show you, and then Grandmother says we can go down to the village and I can introduce you to the twins! Isn't that a marvellous prospect for the day ahead?"

It was clear to me that he'd been awake for ages. Not only was he fully dressed, but he certainly seemed to me the type of person to be up and raring to go as soon as possible.

"Come on, come on!" he urged. "Get dressed, let's go – I'll meet you downstairs in five minutes!"

And with that, he was gone.

I stood motionless for a while, staring at the closed door, realising that I was still smiling. Alphie certainly did have that kind of effect.

I knelt next to my suitcase and quickly pulled out some jeans and a T-shirt for what promised to be a busy day. I pulled them on quickly, remembering that I hadn't yet washed. I didn't mind: adventure left little room for hygiene.

Stuffing my feet into the slippers and scrunching up my toes in a declaration of my belonging, I walked out of my room and into the circular landing. I must have turned in a full circle before I remembered which door we had come through the previous night.

I climbed out from behind the tapestry covering the door, less gracefully than I would have liked, and crept through the creaking corridors and past the piercing portraits, as the sound of the gong signalled that I was already late to breakfast.

"Were those your sweet, sweet footsteps I heard?"

Definitely Alphie.

"Come on, I'm waiting for you down here!"

***

Azariah

Emilie went downstairs and ate breakfast as if her last meal were a lifetime ago. Alphie babbled non-stop and Emilie listened happily – she had never met anyone with such an apparent energy for life, and his excitement was reflected in the glint of her eyes. Breakfast had been on the table when she appeared in the doorway – eggs and soldiers – her favourite. She hadn't got a clue how Alphie had known they were her favourite, she didn't even know if he had been the one to make breakfast, but she knew that she was hungry enough for the food to stop her questions for the time being.

It was lucky she hadn't asked Alphie though. Little white lies aren't exactly his strong point.

Meanwhile, Etty was on her weekly visit to me, but I won't disclose any further information on that particular subject right now. I did promise you that I'm not just some strange spirit spying on Emilie, I have been commissioned by Etty specifically to watch over her. And I don't know about you, but Emilie would have found that marvellously thrilling.

When they finished their breakfast, Alphie decided it was time for the all-important tour. They decided to start outside while the weather remained fair and made their way to the mammoth wooden doors at the front of the house. It took a joint effort, both pulling with all their might, before the doors opened with a creak that promised adventure ahead. Stepping out into the light of the morning, Alphie grabbed Emilie's hand and raced across the front of the old manor. They turned the corner and Alphie stopped abruptly in his tracks, as if halted by the most powerful of spells. Emilie stared. Enchanted.

It was the breath-taking view she had seen from her

window, but from a completely new perspective. Those little streaks of green and blue in her eyes seemed to grow as she gazed across the vista; her ears focussed on the pummelling of waves and on the cry of seagulls from afar. She stuck her tongue out to taste the bitterness of the air and the crispy scent of the sea. The wind whipped around her face, throwing her hair in every direction and filling her with a fervour that she had never felt before. She spread out her arms and lifted her face to the sky.

And although Emilie didn't know it, Alphie was staring right back at her with the same expression of impressed wonderment.

***

Emilie

Alphie must have thought I was completely ridiculous, for my little show in the garden, but I didn't care one bit.

After exploring the outside, Alphie invited me on a grand tour of the manor, avoiding, of course, the top floor. As we passed the stairs towards it, I got a chill of excitement. However, Alphie evaded my questions – I got the feeling he didn't actually know what was up there but wanted to keep the impression of an all-knowledgeable host. I smiled to myself and allowed him to continue the tour, putting aside the notion of the top floor for the time being. Besides, there were plenty of other adventurous things to see. Sadly, we didn't stumble into any secret passageways. I was convinced there had to be some in a house like this, but Alphie didn't seem to know of any and my hips were beginning to feel quite sore from bumping into walls in the hope that they might give way to doors. Still, we entered many dust-covered rooms and it was enough to imagine what they might have been like in the olden days: ladies' skirts swishing through piles of books, laughter and tobacco filling the air.

By the time we had finished our tour, the soles of my feet cried out for a break, but Alphie had other ideas.

We headed out to meet his friends at one o'clock and as we closed the large wooden doors behind us, the wind picked up, as if in spite. We trudged inland down the cliff, collars turned up – even Alphie's mouth was closed against the wind. Past the gates the land seemed less groomed: hedges and trees sprouted at intervals in a rather careless manner. But even among the madness there seemed to be a method to it – an almost comforting type of craziness.

It began to drizzle as we continued along the road. There were few cars and even less noise. We must have been walking for at least half a mile and the drizzle was, if anything, growing, making me begin to feel as if the dampness had become a part of me. Then, as we came to the top of a hill, I spotted a village, nestled in the valley against the rain. It had perhaps only fifteen or twenty buildings, but each one was lit up, like candles flickering in the wind.

"Come on," called Alphie, over the weather.

We came to the first house, a little cottage, complete with a beautiful head of thatched hair, just like something from one of the fairy tales I loved. The road then split off at an old war memorial and we took the left path passing three or four more cottages, before arriving at a small village green. Circling it I could see a tiny post-office, a pub, a bank, a church and a village shop, the letters displaying the supermarket chain rather ruining the quaintness of it all. Each sat proud in their position and passing all these, we reached another cottage, where Alphie finally slowed. A faint echo of laughter sounded from within.

Some scuffling followed Alphie's knock, before the door was opened by a boy about my age. He had the most beguiling grin stretched across his dark brown face and tight locks coiled around his head. A baby girl was precariously placed over one hip.

"Alphie!" he beamed, eyes sparkling. I couldn't help but notice a dimple marking his left cheek, as if worn in by a wonky smile. Without waiting for a reply, he yelled over his shoulder. "Lori! Alphie and Emilie are here!"

A girl soon appeared at the door and quickly took her place next to the boy, who was evidently her twin. The girl had cornrows leading into two long, braided pigtails, which reached her hips in a way that made me immediately envious. Both her cheeks sported little dimples; her smile evidently more evenly spread than her brother's.

"Do come in out of the cold and the wet." The girl's voice was confident and melodious. "My name is Lori and this is my twin Zander."

"Yep, and before you make the mistake - Lori is short for Lorelai not Lauren and she must have it pronounced Lor-el-i not Lor-el-ay or Lor-el-ee although for some odd reason she insists her nickname must be pronounced Lor-ee," Zander declared in a seemingly well-rehearsed line, while winking at his sister, who in return gave him a mock irritated look.

I followed the three down the hall, through a low door and into the kitchen, suddenly feeling a little out of place. The kitchen would have been considered large, were it not for the rather elongated dining-room table and all the people bustling around its centre. The noise was what hit me. From behind Alphie, I could see a boy and a girl in a corner squabbling over a teddy of some sorts, whilst a very pretty girl, who seemed about ten, was trying to stop them. Over the oven leant a woman of skirts, whose hips swayed in comfortable rhythm to the beat of the radio – definitely their mother. Zander placed the baby, who was busy burbling away to an invisible imagining of her young mind, on the kitchen-top beside the woman, safely out of reach of the oven and the edge. I had never been in a room with so much noise or so many children and I felt temporarily stunned.

As I entered the room the children in the corner stopped bickering and turned to stare at me. Sensing the quiet their mother turned, beaming.

"Emilie," she said in a voice similar to Lori's, yet deepened by years of motherhood, "we've been expecting you; Etty said you'd be coming for lunch." Her smile, although unfamiliar, and the smells of home cooking, although unlike any I'd ever smelt before, reminded me of my mum and for a second a pang of homesickness threatened to overwhelm me.

Turning to Alphie with a sweep, she took him in her arms and looked him up and down, smothering him in her maternal layers.

"Well it's good to see Etty's been feeding you, I hope you haven't been getting into any trouble lately."

"Me in trouble, Mrs Sanders?" he said in a disbelieving voice, removing himself from her apron. "Never!"

At that moment another two people descended on the chaos of the room. A man of incredible height, whom I assumed to be their father, and a boy of about seventeen, whose large round glasses circled his midnight eyes.

"Just in time," Mrs Sanders said with a smile. "Everybody to the table please."

A cacophony of squeaking chairs and clattering dishes ensued, as the radio was turned off and the food was brought to the table. I followed shyly as Alphie laughingly guided me to a seat between him and Lori. The food was served and Alphie was soon deep in conversation with Zander to his left, and once again I felt a little lost as five or more conversations ensued

33

across the table. Lori left little time for me to feel that way though, as she turned to me and asked whether I was able yet to understand Alphie's vocabulary. I replied in a whisper that it had been rather confusing me.

"I would say you'll get used to it, but it has been puzzling me for the past five years, so I don't want to get your hopes up!"

I laughed and recalled to her the way he had introduced himself to me, to which she rolled her eyes, giggling.

"Classic," she replied as in turn she told me many of the crazy things he had said over the years. Together we dissolved in giggles and were forced to drop the conversation and return to our food as Alphie turned towards us with a quizzical look. The food was a delicious creamy kind of stew which I was informed was in fact a soup – egusi soup. I loved the name and I thought how much more exciting it was than my mum's classic pasta bake. I felt a little guilty for the thought.

Mrs Sanders brought us into a larger conversation as she questioned what Alphie and I had been up to that morning. Alphie told her of our exploration and Idara, the girl who had been trying to calm the earlier scuffle, suggested a massive game of hide and seek in the manor for another day. I was a little disappointed that I hadn't thought of the idea.

I struggled to keep up with all their names. Fabian was the eldest and Alesha was the baby, whose gurgles punctured our conversation. The other two I struggled to recall, and it wasn't until the food was finished and the little girl walked around the table to sweetly inquire if she could sit on my lap that Alphie quietly reminded me her name was Aretta. With Aretta on my lap, Mrs Sanders left to put Alesha to sleep and, on her return, we began a rather long game of two truths one lie, an apparent favourite for when they had new guests. Visi, the final child whose name I'd forgotten, had my favourite three statements: he'd lit a candle, he'd been swimming, or he'd been arrested. Out of pity Lori guessed the first, Zander guessed the second, though that was more for humour. I was of course right in guessing the third.

We ended up staying the whole afternoon, settling down for a game of Monopoly in the living room after lunch. Zander was the most ridiculous monopoly player I'd ever seen, and I wondered whether he simply didn't understand the rules, or rather took delight in twisting them. Either way, his antics kept us entertained, and on occasion in hysterics. I felt I was able to get really close to Lori over the game; she seemed to be the kind of person who would make friends with anyone wherever she went, and I was glad we got along so well. We even teamed up to utterly bankrupt the boys. Lori and I chatted for hours afterwards, although I honestly couldn't remember half of the things we talked about. Tea and toast over their fire perfectly ended our visit and we left with promises to meet up again the next day.

***

Azariah

I watched Alphie and Emilie walk back in high spirits,
Alphie whistling a tune, and I knew from experience
why. The family had an off-beat tempo to them that was
undeniably infectious. I was pleased to see that Emilie
had been able to make friends with them so quickly,
they're good friends of mine too. My hope was that their
open heartedness and good nature would be reflected
more and more in Emilie, and that which Etty feared
wouldn't come to pass.

CHAPTER THREE

Emilie

*B*y the time we got back to the manor (doesn't that sound wonderful!) it was growing dark. There was some supper left in the kitchen which Alphie and I guiltily prodded, still rather full from the big meal at lunch. Alphie continued his usual chatter over the food and all the way to our tower, but I was too busy thinking to pay him much attention – not that he seemed to notice.

Being back in the manor, my imagination was even more electrified than last night, now being stripped of all nervousness I'd felt at the start. I knew I had felt foolish that morning when I had opened the chest and expected to find something adventurous, and that I was disappointed that we hadn't found any secret passages that morning, but I couldn't shake the idea that there was something mysterious underlying this place. More than anything, Etty's warning against the top floor had planted that forbidden area firmly in my mind. Now it was bubbling, brought alive by my imaginings of all that might await. Perhaps Etty had a mad husband kept in the attic, like Bertha in that book I had stolen from Lizzie's shelf; perhaps that was where all of the maps and secret passageways were, instead of in a trunk in my room. Not that Lizzie would ever believe in such a thing as a real-life Bertha.

A plan was forming in my head. It was getting late, and Aunt Etty's rooms didn't seem to be anywhere near here…

"Alphie," I whispered urgently (this occasion seemed to call for whispering). We had stopped at my door and Alphie had opened it for me with a ridiculous flourish and bow.

"Yes," he replied, matching my tone.

"Why don't you know what's on the top floor?"

"Oh," he replied in a louder voice, breaking the thrill of the moment, "I guess I never felt the particular necessity to. I did mention it once and Grandmother said she was awaiting the right time to chance upon us. Besides, I learnt the hard way that it isn't worth disobeying Grandmother."

The idea of 'the right time' only thrilled my curiosity all the more.

"Have you never wondered what's up there?"

"Sure I have, but I'm not one to give in to rampant curiosity."

With that he smiled, as if telling me that the conversation was over, and went to leave my room. But before he could I managed: "Well I am, and I'm going to explore. Meet me back here at midnight, otherwise I'm going alone."

All this was said in a violent whisper, and to emphasise my point, I grabbed the door handle from him and shut it myself, leaving poor Alphie outside. The satisfying click of the lock supported the seriousness of my statement. I could imagine Alphie's raised eyebrow from behind the door, surprised at my sudden outburst. I felt a little uncomfortable about being so forceful and was stung for a second by the worry that I had scared him away. But somehow, I was sure that come midnight he would be standing outside my door waiting. He wouldn't want to let me down, even a single day of knowing him had shown me that much.

I decided that, since before most adventure stories the hero gets some rest, I would try to. But, like many of the said heroes, I could not.

I lay awake for many time-warped hours, staring into the eyes of the painted couple opposite me. What had seemed enchanting in the light of the morning, now began to morph into some sinister scheme of darkness. I rolled over to turn from the painting, peering at my watch. 10:06. *Was it really only half an hour since we had gone to bed?* I had picked midnight because it had seemed the most dramatic time for an adventure, but it felt like midnight would never come. I realised then why many storybook characters are tossed into an adventure: because the waiting is boring for those who go searching for their adventures at midnight.

By 11:50, time had slowed beyond the bearable. I rolled out of bed, carefully avoiding the seemingly disapproving eyes of the paint-stroke couple, pulled on my dressing gown and slippers, and left the room, silently drawing the door closed. Alphie wasn't there. *Yet.*

It was at 11:58, when I was teetering on the edge of giving up, that Alphie's door peeked open. The sigh of relief collapsed my nerves as he appeared. Adventures are always better with a partner, especially nighttime ones, I had learnt that much last night. Alphie didn't look like he had slept much either, and his uncharacteristic silence told me he was a little grumpy. Yet he still managed to throw a smile in my direction.

"Come on then, let's get this over with."

They were not the precise words I would have chosen to introduce an adventure, but I silently forgave him with enormous maturity, and together we opened the door to leave the circular landing.

I was once more confronted with the house at night, once more had to walk down the corridor of ancestors, who seemed distant by day, but strangely awakened at night. I was glad when Alphie slipped his hand into mine. The corridors were long, my imagination wild, my heart pounding. Alphie had suggested turning back at least eight times by the time we reached the stairs to the top floor. I had pulled him roughly on, annoyed at him for spoiling the seriousness of the moment. But when we came to stand at the foot of the steps leading to the top floor, I was almost tempted to listen to his plea to turn back. *What if Etty's mad husband really was up there?* We hadn't brought anything to defend ourselves with and neither of us were exactly an icon of physical strength. But we couldn't turn back now. It would be far too anti-climactic. I grasped Alphie's hand tighter, the warmth reassuring me. He turned to see determination steeling in my eyes, and together we began to ascend the stairs…

The stairs were simple, wooden and narrow, like the stairs you might get in a barn house, not an ancient manor. I took a deep breath with every step, steeling myself to run back down to the tower should we find anything with the potential to eat us. It was, therefore, quite a shock to be met not by iron-clad cages holding savage half-humans or rattling chains or feral animals but by a plushily carpeted corridor with handleless doors on either side, dimly visible through flickering candlelight.

"Eight, ten, twelve, thirteen," I heard Alphie count beside me. Thirteen doors.

In a way the simplicity and normality of the corridor was more terrifying. Why didn't Etty want us up here? What secrets were being kept behind these doors? I knew the sensible thing would be to go back to bed and forget all about this mysterious corridor – that would be what Lizzie would encourage me to do, but I knew I wouldn't be able to just forget the corridor. It would drive me mad, and I knew in my heart that I would only end up here again if I turned back now. It was best to adventure now, whilst Alphie was there with me, and adrenaline was high in both our bodies.

A glimpse at Alphie showed me that he felt the same – we'd come too far to turn back now. He seemed to have gained courage from the realisation that there was nothing here that could eat us. *Yet*. My dad had always encouraged me to add 'yet' to the end of sentences, and this seemed like a thrilling, if scary, time to do so.

In silent agreement, Alphie and I tiptoed to the first door on our right, a sensible place to start – not too far from the stairs should anything alive emerge. However, now my thoughts had turned more towards treasure. Perhaps Etty was involved in a group of coastal smugglers, and this was their lair. She didn't strike me as someone involved in illegal affairs, but appearances could be deceptive.

"What do you think is in there?" I whispered to Alphie.

"I really don't know, but I'm hoping for answers to some long-held questions I have," was his rather thrilling reply. I wanted to question him on this further, but every second we stood outside the door I could feel my anticipation grow.

"On the count of three," I whispered.

"One, two, three." We both thrust our hands forward with held breath and collided with the door.

It was locked.

We shoved again, harder this time, but with no more success. I turned to the door behind us and gave it a kick, hoping that maybe that one would move. I merely stubbed my toe and drew back wincing. We tried the next two just to be sure, but they also refused to budge, and their lack of handles meant that there wasn't even a lock to attempt to pick – I had brought a hairpin along just in case.

The original hush, holding of breath and hands, bracing of courage and shoulders,1 was repeatedly met with frustration: we failed to open any of the doors we tried even an inch.

However, as we headed down the corridor, something strange began to happen. At the second set of doors a hum began, unnoticeable to begin with, but distinctly louder the further down we went. It was like the hum of an upstairs hoover, not imposing but impossible to ignore. The humming throbbed through my imagination until it was all that I could hear or think of, and I located it coming from the door on the right, two before the end.

I questioned Alphie on the source of the humming, but he seemed just as confused as me.

"Well, we should probably try the door it's coming from." Alphie nodded, although I could tell he was beginning to waver. I walked and placed my ear against the door it was coming from, expecting Alphie to do the same. So, it was to my astonishment that Alphie turned to the left instead and shoved his ear against a door opposite me. We turned and faced each other, confusion mirrored on both our faces.

"The humming is definitely coming from this door!" I insisted. I had heard it grow to vibrations as I approached, unmistakable now.

"I distinctly hear it from mine," Alphie retorted. "Look, this is all very peculiar, don't you reckon it would be better to return tomorrow when it's lighter and we've had some more time to contemplate on the matter?" he continued.

But logic could not reach me now, instead it irritated me. Could he not feel the pull to the door? The pull to the humming? The pull to discovery and adventure?

"Fine, you go. I'm opening this door."

Alphie lifted his hands in helplessness, I think he knew it would be fruitless to argue with me now.

I stood outside my chosen door, heartbeat building, Alphie looking on.

"On the count of three. One. Two. Three."

I pushed and, soundlessly and with no effort at all, the door swung open. Sharing a triumphant look with Alphie, I stepped inside.

The door pulled to behind me and I was enveloped by light. Sweetened, golden light that seemed to enclose the room, filling the floors and walls and ceiling, calling me, drawing me in. I couldn't see anything else but the light, as walls and ceiling seemed to disappear, and I wondered for a second whether I really had entered a room. I couldn't see or sense an end to the space, but nor did it seem to continue on. Confusion tingled in my mind as a physical warmth tingled on my skin, and I knew I should have been blinded by the light, but instead my eyes seemed to have been opened to a sense superior even to sight. The light seemed to fill me and grow inside me, pulsing through my veins and seeping into my every bone, making me feel more alive than any amount of blood flow could ever do. It felt like home. But unlike any home I had ever entered, like a bigger and better home that no simple house could provide. And I felt more myself than I ever had before; not that I wasn't myself normally. It didn't make sense in the slightest, but somehow it made more sense to me than anything else ever had.

Then the whispers started, whispers that thrilled and filled me just as the light had done, but in a different way – in a terrifying way that made my blood vibrate rather than pulse. The whispers grew in size. A woman's voice. A man's voice. Tiny tendrils of darkness pushed forward into the light and the voices seemed to come from within it, drawing me to them, as they twisted around me, fighting to block out the light. And in a way I wanted to follow, to go further into the room, to explore the darkness just as I had the light.

But a sharp pain and a tug, coming from behind,

pulled me back.

Pulled me out.

The door slammed behind me, and I fell to the floor of the forbidden top floor, looking up into the eyes of the last person I wanted to see.

CHAPTER FOUR

Emilie

Enough," commanded Aunt Etty, "I'm doing this properly before someone gets hurt. Follow me."

"What, you're telling her already? I thought you said -" Alphie blurted out, before being silenced by a glance from Aunt Etty.

"You've left me no choice."

And before I could confess to the size of my part in our adventure, I was pulled to my feet by the firmest of hands, and Etty's look silenced me too.

I mouthed a small apology to Alphie, and he rewarded me a small smile in return, assuring me that he held nothing against me, although I still felt bad for getting him into trouble with his grandmother.

Alphie and I obediently followed Etty down the staircase in a silence that hid a thousand blaring questions. What I had seen was completely unexplainable, and to be perfectly honest, kind of scary. I had that gut-wrenching feeling of dangling off a cliff edge as I desperately tried to think of something that could explain all I had seen and felt and heard in an attempt to secure myself on known ground. But it was no use. My imagination was once again running rapidly out of control, dreaming up adventures and startling new worlds and foreseeing previously hidden colours, trying to somehow place the mysterious light and dark within it.

But then I remembered that this wasn't a fantasy in my head. This was real. Undoubtedly real, because in my dreams I had never felt scared. These sorts of things never *actually* happened. Things like the light and dark and shadows of the room I had entered were normally walled in by the figments of my imagination, encaged by the tales of fictional characters. Whenever I dreamt up a situation of such sorts, I had never been blocked by a fear that physically stopped my brain from thinking. I had never been so unnerved that my hands shook. And I had never wanted so much for the world to slow down and stop spinning, so that my head could stop spinning along with it.

I was used to urging time to speed up, to seeing fairies where only shadows played. For the first time I begged there to be a reasonable explanation, not a fantastical story awaiting a narrator. But why else would I have felt such a surge of energy a few minutes ago in the room? I could still feel the remains of that surge in the form of a tingling in my gut. I clenched my hands to my belly as we entered the kitchen and didn't release them until Alphie and I were seated on the bench opposite Aunt Etty.

"Magic," stated Aunt Etty, matter-of-factly, and then paused.

I was so taken aback that even my brain ceased its fizzling of questions. The way she spoke, with that blunt practicality, left no room for doubt. Of course, I had often pretended with my sister that magic was real, acting out stories from fairy tales together. But Lizzie had never believed in it herself. In fact, she had always tried to talk me out of that 'nonsense', although she would eventually give in and play along for my sake. I wondered how she would react to Aunt Etty's statement. I squeezed my eyes tight and tried to imagine it, tried to react as Lizzie would so I could appear mature in front of Alphie.

But I knew I wouldn't be able to. My family had all been surprised when I refused to stop playing make-believe, blaming it on my 'overactive imagination', although of course by the time I got to secondary school, I knew how to play my games in secret. And now my aunt wanted me to continue the game with her. I thought the age of twelve was too old for all that, let alone the age of twelve hundred (or however old she was).

"So, what is magic, in your mind, Emilie?" Aunt Etty asked.

I was so confused by the question that I stuttered for a couple of moments before managing to spurt out: "What – like fairies and witches?!"

"No," she replied coldly, and then went silent, staring at me with this disappointed look on her face. It made me squirm with the uselessness of my answer. If it was some kind of test to see how level-headed I was, I had clearly failed.

Alphie came to my rescue, having obviously regained himself somewhat.

"It's just things we can't explain, isn't it?" he hinted to me. His eyes were filled with the warmth of encouragement. My look of confusion must have conveyed I hadn't a clue what he was talking about. He turned to Etty as if for permission to explain, and she nodded. He continued slowly, clearly dumbing down his language for me. "For example, if a wizard points a wand at something and makes it do something without touching it, then everyone believes that must be magic."

"I guess so," I replied. I didn't have a clue where he was going with this.

"But if I point a remote control at something and make *it* do something without touching it, everyone understands that it's technology. We know how it works. But what's the only difference between the two examples? One we understand, and the other we don't. One we can explain, so we say its technology. The other we can't explain and so we say it's magic. But we only say it's magic because we don't understand how it works *yet*. And the 'yet' is very important." My mind immediately flitted back to my dad. *Could he have been preparing me for this, whatever 'this' is?*

Was Alphie being serious? Was he truly trying to explain the existence of something bigger than physics and logic? It was all I could do to keep up with the line of his explanation.

"Because if you took someone from the medieval times and showed them the wizard with his wand and me with my remote control, they would think both were magic. So, one day when we understand how the 'magic' wizard uses his wand, it won't be magic anymore. The more we can explain, the less 'magic' there is in this world. So, either everything's magic, or nothing's magic, depending on how you perceive it."

"Yes - if it actually existed, that is," I spluttered. Aunt Etty sighed.

"You're missing the point!" Alphie said, now a little frustrated. "Let's skip the part where you can't believe it all and get straight to the important bits."

I felt like a smoke bomb had exploded in my chest. *Skip the part where I can't believe?*

"You mean to pretend it's all real?" I questioned, hesitant, my mind numbed by bewilderment. "Suspend my disbelief? Pretend all the childhood fairy tales are real?"

Alphie seemed a little irritated. "Look, we're simply *never* going to get through this explanation if you keep stopping when you think something sounds

51

impossible."

Etty had been eagling me the whole time Alphie was talking. Her face was rocky with seriousness. It was like they were reciting lines from a play and were about to break out of character at any minute.

"A long time ago," Aunt Etty started, "people began to notice that some children were being born with special powers. Some could control time or space, some could change the weather, others had control over minds and so on. But each child only had one power. And soon it was noticed that there were twelve main powers in existence, correlating strongly between the months of these children's birthdays. January babies had the power of sight. February babies had the power over an aspect of an element. March gave babies the power of weather, and so on. These powers were inherited down the family line, and these people became known as the Potensa."

"Now," she said, looking me right in the eye, "I need you to think back to all the fairy tales you were told as a child. Think of witches, wizards, fairies and elves."

I could barely think at all. "They don't really exist, do they?" The words toppled out of my mouth.

"Of course not!" Alphie snorted. Despite myself, I felt a little stab of disappointment.

"That's the whole point," Etty continued. "Of course fairies and wizards don't exist – not as the legends portray them anyway – they're just all Potensa."

Potensa? The word rolled about my mind, formed on my tongue. But I couldn't make my lips move an inch.

Aunt Etty continued, "Fairy tales exist because of the Potensa. Thousands of years ago it was understood perfectly well that these people existed, but they fell into legend and folklore, as is the way of magical things. The name Potensa was lost to history and replaced with the term fairy. They became what you know today from your stories."

"So, the stories got it wrong? Each one of these … Potensa only has one power, according to which month they were born in?" I could barely believe the words my own mouth was uttering.

"Yes," said Aunt Etty definitively.

Alphie coughed awkwardly and stared at his feet, but I had no time to question it.

"Okay…" I thought aloud. "I think I understand." I didn't quite, but I knew what I had to ask. "So … what does it have to do with me? Are you about to tell me that you and I are part of these Potensa people?" I held my breath, unable to seize the enormity of what I was asking. Could I really be about to discover I was special after all? Was something much crazier than any of my wildest dreams about to happen to me?

Aunt Etty ignored my question and continued with her explanation. "A couple of centuries ago, the Potensa started dying out. Certain Ordinaries – that's someone who's not a Potensa – began to think they could kill a Potensa to take their power. The few Ordinaries who knew about us were quick to betrayal when this false rumour spread. Trusted friends of Potensa, or even powerless spouses of Potensa, began to capture and kill our people."

Our people. My ears buzzed with thrills.

"The Potensa stopped knowing whom to trust. They began to be afraid of having children, fearing they would not be strong enough to protect their offspring against these monsters who would kill them for their power. And of course, killing a Potensa could never transfer a power from them to an Ordinary, no matter how many different ways the Ordinaries tried. They killed so many of us, over so many years, we were in danger of losing everything. But there is a way to preserve the powers and keep the magical gene alive."

"Wait, what?" Alphie exploded. This was obviously news to him too.

"Your great great great great great great grandfather – eight generations ago – came up with the solution. He found a way to channel a power from a living Potensa into a special room, a special room called a Rhisa. Working with one Potensa from each month, and thereby with all twelve powers, he set out to establish the strongest of protective and defensive charms around each room, around each Rhisa. Together, they built one Rhisa for each power, as a source and storage space for them. That means that although there may be fewer Potensa now, each one is stronger than ever before as they can train and replenish their power using their Rhisa, drawing on the strength of Potensa who have gone before them. When they are old enough and strong enough, they can go and channel some power back into the rooms, ready for the next generation of Potensa to use."

"So that's what we found?" I almost shouted, practically frothing and seething with wonder and excitement.

"Yes, you did. Not quite in the way I anticipated, but that can't be helped now. You wandered into the Rhisa of Light."

I held my breath. Alphie was beaming at me.

"And that, my dearest girl, is your power."

***

Azariah

I watched the whole thing. Having spent her entire life dreaming up adventures of magic and fantasy, you would have thought Emilie would be the first to accept something unbelievable. But the way I see it, the more you dream about something, the less likely it seems when it actually happens. So as Alphie and Etty began to talk to Emilie about magic, I watched her face as mystery flickered to confusion, and confusion fluttered to amazement.

But I knew Etty hadn't quite told her the whole story. Now was not the moment.

The most amusing spectacle by far was the look on Alphie's face as Etty spun her tale. I could just about see each thought flashing through his mind. That meant he was growing dearer to Emilie – I'm best at reading those closest to her.

Naturally, Alphie knew about the Potensa, but I can assure you he had never stumbled across the Rhisa before in all his years of living with her, having never disobeyed his grandmother's words before. I suppose you could say that Emilie was a bad influence on him. But the damage was already done. Etty had seen it coming for a long time and, in a peculiar way, she later confided in me, she was glad it had happened when it did.

And so, as she told of the magical Rhisa, and their great great great great great great grandfather, Alphie's eyes grew in moon-sized surprise just as much as Emilie's did. The excitement of sharing a wondrous secret morphed into the excitement of discovering one himself, and he was practically shaking with questions by the time Etty was finished.

"So that was Emilie's Rhisa we chanced upon!" he blurted out. "Where's mine? Is it the last one? Can we go back up now? Please?!"

"All in good time," responded Etty, matching his agitation with an equal dose of composure. "You should know better than anyone that such things mustn't be rushed."

Indeed, the pitfalls of rushing 'such things' were evident enough from the look on Emilie's face as she embraced the news of the Potensa: eyebrows fixed in raised stupefaction, mouth open in widened bewilderment, her bottom lip quivering with unuttered questions. Seeing her hypnotic state, Alphie managed to calm down (at least I could tell he was trying his best to) enough to remember that it was a lot for his cousin to take in, and he mustn't demand his grandmother to reveal even more.

There is no proper response to these sorts of things, and, in my lifetime, I have seen every variation. Some cry, some scream, and some register themselves with a psychiatric organisation almost immediately. Most Potensa are brought up in magical families of course, and so never know any different. If you tell a child under the age of five, they will generally accept it readily. Emilie, luckily, was still under twenty, at which point 'common sense' and 'logic' make any transition to the Potensa lifestyle extremely challenging. But nonetheless, I think it's fair to say she was rather shaken up, the roots of her imagination having been overturned and exposed.

Things rarely turn out the way we imagine them. Perhaps that's why Emilie was more reluctant to accept who she was. Her brain tricked her into assuming she was dreaming, or crazy, or perhaps even that she was dead. Even with her quirky over-dramatic nature, I could tell Emilie was inclined to believe this was too much like something from a film to be true.

"But I don't have any magical powers!" she insisted.

"But you're adopted, right?" replied Alphie.

"You've never been taught how to access it, that's all," said Etty, speedily shutting down Alphie's train of thought. "And around Ordinaires you wouldn't have felt it lurking much within. But you are old enough now to learn the truth, that's why I requested your parents send you here for the summer.

"My parents? My parents knew I was a Potensa?!"

"Yes, of course, that's why they sent you here. And now I can show you. That feeling you experienced upstairs; that surge of power, that can be tamed and used. If you're ready and willing, of course."

I've never seen Emilie nod her head so vigorously in her entire life.

CHAPTER FIVE

Emilie

I could barely believe it. And yet, in a strange way, it kind of made sense. Neither my wildest dreams nor my craziest hopes could have convinced me that this was happening in real life. But there wasn't much to do other than accept it.

So, I did. Then came the questions. Lots of questions. It was hard to sit still through their answers. I wanted to know it all, but I wanted even more to be able to use my power.

I honestly didn't have a clue what to expect next.

The sun was rising when I began to feel like I had wrapped my head around the basics at least.

"I probably should send you two back to bed," Aunt Etty told us. "Exploring is tiring work, particularly when it's without permission." Her tone was stern, if tinged with a shade of humour.

Alphie and I hung our heads, ready to accept whatever lecture was to come. But Aunt Etty laughed at the sorry look on our faces. "I doubt you would be able to sleep though. So, if you are ready, we'll get right to it. No need to dilly-dally." And with that, she strode out of the room. I daggered a raised eyebrow at Alphie, hopped off my chair, and ran after her.

Rather than heading back up to the Rhisa like I expected, Aunt Etty went out through the hall and to the massive front door. Heaving it open, she exited into the bright world outside. The morning was cool, and the dew heavy, but through the first light of the sun, dusting the ground with morning rays, and through the light of my new-found knowledge, I was able to take in for the first time how unusual our surroundings were. Where else would there be a mansion, on the edge of a cliff, in the middle of absolutely nowhere? But instead of hurrying down the drive, Aunt Etty looped around the back of the house. We started off on a gravel footpath which hugged the exterior walls of the old house, a path I now noted that Alphie and I had not explored the day before. Around and around we followed, without a word passing between us. Aunt Etty was in the lead, maintaining a surprisingly fast pace. Behind her hurried Alphie, and I was hot on his footsteps, practically running to keep up with the mysterious duo.

The manor wasn't exactly square, largely due to the strangely flung extensions and the many nooks and crannies which the footpath followed. But even so, it seemed like we were going around the house for an eternity. Okay, maybe that's a bit of an exaggeration. But there was simply far too much wall. The exterior walls started off as panels of clean-shaven bricks. But soon the bricks grew older, the cracks widened like wrinkles and my confusion aged in equal measure. *Surely the house wasn't this large?* I tried to remember back to the tour Alphie gave me yesterday. No, it definitely hadn't seemed this large yesterday, though we hadn't gone down this path.

And yet still Aunt Etty was hurrying down the gravel footpath at an alarming speed. Alphie seemed completely content at the morning's unexpected outcome, stroking past the increasingly faded bricks as he went. It seemed only I was at a loss, though I suppose the supernatural shape of the house wasn't the most surprising thing of that day. At any moment I expected us to arrive back at the front, and yet one wall just led to another.

After another few minutes though, I spotted what appeared to be the corner of the house. A large archway formed from a bush nestled against the end of the exterior wall. The gravel path stopped decisively short of its opening, and the gardens to the right merged into a thicket of squabbling brambles. I couldn't make any sense of it. I wondered whether perhaps this was the other side of the house. Maybe through the arch we'd reappear near the front door.

Quite suddenly, Aunt Etty stopped in her tracks and I thought for a second that she too was lost.

"Look carefully at this archway," she commanded. I did, but there didn't seem to be anything of particular note about it. It curved a ripened dome of leaves, a foot or two taller than my head, and the archway was so long I struggled to see the other end of it. Alphie was sporting a comically large grin on his face as I inspected it.

"This," started Aunt Etty with a grandeur I immediately loved, "Is the Darwala." (I could tell it had a capital D from the way she said it.)

"The Darwala is an ancient entrance that not just anyone can get through," she continued, "only Potensa."

It felt momentous, standing there with the gateway to another world right in front of me. It was hard to believe that this even existed, let alone that it was right behind Aunt Etty's house. Or were we around the front now?

For a magical portal it seemed remarkably average. Mysterious, perhaps, but certainly not supernatural. But then, as if it could hear my thoughts, the leaves near the entrance of the arch started to shimmer. Aunt Etty took flight again and charged (if an old lady can charge) down through the archway. Alphie followed in hot pursuit. Leaving me with no choice. I followed, though much more nervously. The sun was stretching through the leaves most lazily, so that even when squinting I couldn't see right the way to the end.

As I stepped underneath, the shimmer of the leaves

became a trembling. I stopped to look up for a second, and when I squinted forwards again, Etty and Alphie were gone. The rays of the sun were unbearable, so I turned around to look back out along the gravel path from which we came. The leaves suddenly stopped vibrating.

What if Aunt Etty was wrong? What if I couldn't get through the passage? Or worst of all, what if they were just playing some horrible prank on me?

For a second, I almost decided it would be better to turn back, to show them I wasn't as gullible as they thought, to show them that their horrible prank hadn't worked after all. But really I was beginning to will this new world, this world of the Potensa, to be proven true. My imagination swung again into motion, dreaming up what could be waiting for me beyond the passageway. It was just about enough to make my head spin and hurtle out of control. I tried to think of Lizzie to calm myself, to imitate her maturity, her level-headedness. But then I realised - there was no place for her level-headedness right now. This was a place for an Emilie, not for a Lizzie.

There was nothing for it. I geared myself up, set on running straight through the archway. Curiosity allows you to do marvellous things, and so, counting down, I ran headfirst under the dome of leaves, eyes pinched tightly shut, and hands running along the edges to steady myself.

When I felt the leaves drop away, I slowed a little,

tottering. My hands brushed air, and I halted altogether.

Breathing heavily from the short sprint, the giddy anticipation and a lack of sleep, I kept my eyes tightly shut, nervous of what I might see when I opened them. What a fool I must have looked like. I could hear sounds of laughter and chatter coming from a distance. Confusion registered. Wasn't it just Alphie and Aunt Etty here? Intrigue instructed my eyes to open. Slowly, as I regained my breath and my courage, I did and was greeted with a reward that even my own outrageous imagination could not have invented.

***

Azariah

I'll admit, it's quite a lot to take in the first time.

After Alphie and Etty came through they whipped around to stare at the Darwala. Waiting. Waiting for the make-or-break moment. It's not designed as a test, and it's not as if we were unsure as to whether Emilie was the real deal or not. But all the same, my heart rose into my throat as we stood there – of course I wasn't going to miss this moment in person – suspended in the lingering pause. Etty seemed outwardly calm, her hands clasped neatly in front of her, but I knew she was clenching her teeth inside. Alphie, on the other hand, looked like a toddler who knew he was about to get a surprise, hopping from foot to foot and begging with his eyes, begging with his every thought, for Emilie to appear.

It took longer than we expected. There was a moment of uncertainty…

And then finally she did.

***

Emilie

It was the most incredible sight. A circus of light and laughter and movement and mayhem. Before me, a small crowd was gathered, Etty and Alphie at the front. It seemed as if they had been waiting for my appearance and the thought inflated my chest with a touch of pride. Clearly no-one else had been worried about me being able to get through the Darwala. I seemed to be on the top of a gentle grassy verge, which sloped down to a desert-flat field expanding right to the cliff edge. Across it, breaking up the green, were what seemed to be hundreds upon hundreds of caravans. Yes, caravans. But they weren't the modern, clinically-white ones. They were more like the typical circus caravans – vibrantly coloured and crookedly shaped – each occupying a spot declared their own. They had little haphazard chimneys, shaped in ways you wouldn't think geometrically possible, twisting and turning like optical illusions and beautiful, intricate paintings adorned their outsides.

The number of caravans packed into the field made me think the edge of the cliff must be miles away, yet from the upstairs window it hadn't seemed so distant. And all around the sides of the field was a hedge that looked to be as tall as the mansion itself. Brambles on the other side of the tunnel melted into it, surrounding the whole field and giving it a feeling of protection. And then there were those people, standing there in an expectant semi-circle, beaming at the look on my face which must have melted from confusion into amazement and been tied up into a bundle of joy. It all made my head hurt a bit.

Alphie wanted to show me everything. The moment Aunt Etty gave her say-so, Alphie was wrenching my hand and yanking me, running, down the hill.

He was everywhere at once, dragging me between the caravans, dodging laundry lines, swerving awnings, and ducking small children on all sides. The camp was packed. There was a real air of excitement encircling the field, spiriting away animated voices from below. Or maybe that was (and I can't believe I'm about to say this!) the MAGIC.

I was out of breath within a few minutes, the wonder of it all as much to blame as Alphie's speed. As we rushed past these homes, a mass of images flashed across my brain. Babies moving rattles without touching them, children disappearing and reappearing in games of tag, mothers heating pots and pans by concentrating the sun's rays into tiny flames. If I didn't believe Aunt

Etty's words fully before, they were being proven absolutely to me now. I couldn't really mistrust my own eyes, could I? A part of me wafted on a breeze above the whole scene, gazing down on the wonder of it all. I felt unconquerable. It was all so astonishing. And yet it didn't feel alien to me at all. I guess you could say I felt like I belonged.

But we were still running through the caravans. I was sure it had been at least ten minutes, but the edge of the cliff didn't seem to be getting any nearer. How that was possible I didn't know, and where we were heading, I could not have guessed either. But by this point a painful stitch was burning up my side. I pulled on Alphie's hand, tugging it, exhausted, and it dropped from his grasp. I groaned, begging him to pause. And as I stood there, bent over, I wondered if in all this magic there was something that gave you a burst of energy, like a stamina pill or something of the sort. *Too hopeful?* I secretly wished Alphie might not notice my absence for a while, so that I might have a couple of moments to breathe, but too soon I felt his hand touch my shoulder. I straightened up, my face flushed and steaming. Alphie's figure stood before me, his mouth turned upwards into a cheeky grin and his eyes fizzing with delight.

Between heaving breaths, I mentioned my ingenious idea of a magical stamina pill, to which he laughed. I guess there were limits to what could be done.

"You, Miss Emilie, are highly out of shape!" he

teased. But we agreed to walk the rest of the way, partially as a small apology for his mocking me. With each breath regained, I unloaded my millions of unanswered questions upon him.

"What is this place?" I puffed, "and why are we here – and where on earth are we going?!"

His response was to tap his nose secretively, and I could only chuckle good-naturedly, although as my face cooled from running, my blood was heating in curiosity.

Eventually we reached one caravan that seemed slightly larger than the others, slightly more crooked in its roof and somewhat more bendy in its walls. Three short sharp raps were delivered by Alphie to the door, and as he did, its sunflowers danced across the paintwork.

"You may find this familiar," Alphie whispered to me as footsteps approached from behind the door.

"TADAAAA!" came a cry as the door was smacked open. My shock must have shown on my face, because the inhabitants burst into hysterical laughter, Alphie along with them. There, perched one above the other, hands stretched out in an excited flourish, were the twins.

"Lori! Zander!" I exploded, jumping up onto the step of the caravan to throw my arms around them. I surprised even myself at such a large gesture, but it was more than a relief to finally recognise something I already knew from this fantastical new world. The twins pulled me down to perch on the steps, while Alphie sat cross-legged before us on the grass. He told me that he had wanted some help in explaining everything to me.

"They're it too, aren't they?" I asked. "They're Potensa people, just like us, right?"

The twins grinned at each other and Lori pointed to a tennis ball lying on the ground, which they both stared at intently. Immediately, it shot up in the air, high above the grass. My eyes traced it, round in wonder.

And my question was answered perfectly.

CHAPTER SIX

Emilie

*T*his cliff can be accessed from anywhere in the world," Zander started, in reply to my long stream of questions. It was actually the first time I'd heard him open his mouth without making a joke. "It never ends. It goes on and on, it only has the illusion of ending in the sea. These caravans aren't all actually here. I mean, they are, obviously, but they're also from everywhere in the world. They're all in two places at once."

I must have pulled a quizzical face because Lori interrupted to help clarify matters slightly.

"It's like a thousand tiny portals," she said, clear and confident. "Each caravan is surrounded by an invisible portal so that it can be in two places at once. Most Potensa families have these caravans – it's a tradition.

That's why they all look like they're hundreds of years old, because they are! Each caravan is connected to two places – this field and the owner's home. They mean that Potensa can gather here without having to travel by boring, normal means."

"Wow," I exhaled. But I was still unsure why everyone would want to round up behind Aunt Etty's manor, for however grassy the field was or however quaint the village, it still wouldn't be my personal choice of a place to park a couple thousand caravans. Lori continued patiently to explain.

"So, when a Potensa family wants to meet or gather with other Potensa, or when your great aunt calls a mass collection, they surround their caravan in a portal, and appear in their assigned lot here. Close the portal and they'll be back at home. It's a very clever system!"

"My aunt calls collections?" I questioned, stumbling over the word "collections" as I attempted to use it correctly.

"Why of course!" replied Zander smiling, "She's the Head at the moment. You know – the Head of all Potensa in Britain. That's why you *had* to know your true origins. That's why you came to stay with her and that's why we're showing you all this."

I thought my head was going to explode with the amount of new information it had been fed that day. Despite my hopes and dreams, I'd never thought that I was actually something special, that I could actually be part of a story or fairy tale. My life had never been anything unique, although I'd spent most of my childhood trying to avoid that fact. But suddenly I felt that I had been let in on the greatest secret in the natural world.

***

Azariah

I watched from afar as Emilie's face lit up, shining with the discovery of the Potensa world. She seemed to me more rounded in expression, as if the unlocking of this secret had completed a part of her she hadn't known was empty. Of course, this wasn't the greatest secret she would ever be informed of, but she didn't know that then. She sat on the steps of that caravan for hours on end as her friends shared their tales.

She learnt that the twins, born on April 1st had the power of telekinesis – the power to move any object they wanted to – and that before they were born their weary mother had thought it would be more than she could bear. They told the often-recited tale of their birth in rehearsed unison, one taking over from the other at the end of each sentence.

"When our mum found out we were due in April," Lori had started, "she knew she'd be in for a handful."

"A pair of twins, able to move things with their minds," Zander had continued with a classic wink.

"It was just about more than she could handle," Lori

laughed.

"And when we came early on the first -" Zander started.

"She knew she had no chance!" they finished in sync.

I know I'm supposed to primarily be watching Emilie, but I couldn't help my attention being drawn to Alphie too during this exchange.

As soon as Emilie had begun asking after her new friends' powers, Alphie's smile had become a little less bright and his enthusiasm had visibly dropped with his shoulders. He'd started to shuffle on the ground, avoiding direct eye contact and pulling out tufts of green from around him. And then Emilie's gaze landed on her cousin. I could just about guess what was going through his head; pity immediately clouded my chest.

"What's your power, Alphie?" I heard her ask good-naturedly, but it was as if her tender tone made him wince. He whipped on a smile immediately, but it wasn't quite reaching his eyes. I was glad she had asked though; it was certainly necessary.

It was Zander who answered for him. "Oh, he's a special one, you know," he teased, trying to help boost past Alphie's expression to keep up the light mood. "He was born on a leap day."

There was silence for a moment, as the children all looked to Alphie, waiting for him to speak. His face didn't give anything away. If only Emilie could understand what I do.

"February 29th," Alphie finally murmured, the

energy in his tone lacking its usual oomph, and then he stopped, offering up no further explanation. His mouth was still upturned but it was beginning to waver. Emilie had never seen him like this before – I could tell it unsettled her.

"It means," prompted Lori, her tone softening as she saw her friend's distress, "that he can control all of the elements. Those born in February are able to control generally one aspect of one element, but leap day babies' powers are unparalleled."

"Or at least they should be." His words were intended to be light-hearted but the bitterness in his voice made it fall flat. "I should go to see if Grandmother needs any help with anything," he murmured, his voice thick with the lie. And before the others could say anything at all, he jumped up, still trying to seem perfectly fine, and ran behind the caravan and out of sight.

I saw the twins exchange worried glances, and the matter hung in the air for a minute before anyone spoke.

"He's supposed to be special, you see," Lori said eventually, "being born on a leap day and all. Only four leap day Potensa ever exist at one time. But he's not very good at harnessing his powers."

"He's not very good – *yet*," Zander corrected her. "He just really feels the pressure, I think. What with him being Etty's grandson and a leap day Potensa, there's a lot of expectation placed on him. He's not very good at being the 'special one'."

Emilie nodded at their words. I could see empathy

swell her chest, could see her decide that she had to find Alphie to talk to him. She excused herself from the twins and walked around the back of the caravan in the direction Alphie had set off in. She found him only a few caravans down, certainly not helping Aunt Etty as he'd said, leaning with his head pressed against a caravan's wall, his feet so far away that his whole body was angled awkwardly against the side. His head was against painted sunflowers which snaked their way around the vehicle's body. Emilie could see now, quite clearly, that the paintings were alive, moving softly around in circles as if blown by a painted wind. A few had gathered around the point at which Alphie's head made contact with the caravan, as if to nuzzle his cares away. I saw Emilie shake off her distraction at yet another piece of magic and walk up behind her cousin so quietly that he barely registered her presence.

"Alphie," she whispered, placing a single hand ever so lightly on his shoulder. "Alphie, it's nothing to be ashamed of."

"I know, I know," he chuckled bravely, straightening up and pulling on a smile at her presence. But Emilie was not done, and her empathy moved me.

"I know nothing – about any of this, which means you can't be worse than me at it. As far as I'm concerned – you're amazing. Whether you can shape-shift, or talk to animals, or control time, or whatever it is you people seem to be able to do – I don't care. I've only known you for a few days and I already think you're pretty fantastic – so there!"

Her confidence made Alphie chuckle more naturally this time. I couldn't be too sure, but I thought I could sense the weight being raised off his chest. He took a few deep breaths and a tiny smile crept into his lips. "I'm sorry to have grown so ungraciously… aggravated," he said, perhaps not quite as playfully as normal, but regaining at least some of his usual brightness. "I just get frustrated at myself sometimes. I feel like I should be better, and I loathe that I'm not. I'll be composed again in a minute."

"We can train together?" Emilie suggested, linking her arm in Alphie's. "I know that I want to learn all there is to learn, so I'm going to need a teacher!"

I watched as the pair walked back to the twins, who immediately showered Alphie with apologies for raising the tricky topic. Alphie had reverted to his usual, enthusiastic self, and swiftly wiped away their apologies with his grandiose style.

I loved watching Emilie grow, watching those moments of gentle kindness. If I had to be assigned to any young Potensa, I'm glad it was her. I was a little worried at first at my assignment, given the 'complications' surrounding her. But so far, she had shown nothing but positive potential.

Emilie

After we cleared up the whole issue with Alphie, I was more desperate than ever to learn more about the Potensa. I didn't really want to ask straight out – not wanting to seem foolish or ignorant – but I was itching to explore.

"So, is there anything else to see then? Anything you can show me?" I finally said, then paused, trying to play off my next sentence casually. "I'm just so excited to explore – you know, it all being new and everything…" I trailed off, scanning their faces for responses.

There was a slight pause, Alphie seemed to be mouthing something to Lori, which she then whispered to Zander, mouth widening around each vowel, and the secrecy of it all made me wriggle with curiosity. Alphie jumped up with a start, grabbing my hand like he had before, and whipped me into the caravan. Lori and Zander leapt in behind us and slammed the door shut.

"You might want to hold onto something," Alphie said, a huge grin lighting his face. The door now bolted, the twins exchanged glances, snapped their fingers twice, and then clapped thrice in unison. The caravan seemed to raise itself slightly in the air as if suspended there, then shuddered back down to the ground with the slightest of bumps. A small heaving sensation rocked my stomach, as it does when a lift accelerates suddenly up a floor.

"Go on then," Zander was smiling at me, "look outside."

I again had that strange mistrusting feeling I'd had when standing at the Darwala, that they could be playing a practical joke on me to make me look silly. But I didn't think Alphie or the twins would do that, not after all I'd just seen. I crept to the door and swung it open.

The field on the cliffside was gone. We were in a back garden.

"We only use it when we're feeling lazy, honest we do!" Lori said. "Aren't you impressed?"

"Is this your back garden?" I asked, staring in astonishment, understanding of the portals finally washing over me.

"Well, it's not Antarctica!" Zander replied triumphantly. "Pretty neat, right?"

We had travelled from the field behind Aunt Etty's to their back garden in the village in a matter of seconds! It made me realise once more how many possibilities were open for Potensa.

"Can we do a more interesting one now?" Alphie asked in a slightly whining tone. "Take us back so we can show Emilie the best ones!"

And before I knew it, within ten seconds, we were back. Alphie reopened the door to the field of caravans, and I was dragged back out the door with the same enthusiasm I had been brought into it. This time, Lori was the one who decided to lead, holding Zander's hand, who was holding my hand in turn. And running beside me was Alphie, who beamed at me as we dashed through the maze of caravans.

I nearly bumped into Zander when he and Lori came to a sudden stop. Zander even pretended to fall over, making Lori roll her eyes, but he squeezed a laugh out from me at least. They'd paused outside a caravan dashed in deep blues and purples. Painted country maidens and farm boys, with beautiful hazel skin flushed from the warmth of the day, chased each other around its exterior, or lazed, watching the brushstroke dusk deepen.

"This one?" Zander asked Alphie and Lori. Receiving nods from both, he knocked politely on its door. The most beautiful girl I had ever seen opened it, complete with the sweetest of smiles. She had every feature I'd ever dreamed of having – eyes the size of walnuts, surrounded by dramatically curled eyelashes which matched her raven hair, and bright cheeks which emphasised her petite nose and lips.

"Can we show our new friend where you come from?" Zander was asking her, clearly struck by her beauty as well, though hiding it better than I was. "This is Emilie – Emilie, this is Maria."

"Do come in, Emilie," she said, her tone as honeyed as her complexion. We all packed into the caravan, and she too snapped twice and clapped thrice – though she did it much more elegantly and less frantically than the twins (if snapping and clapping is something that can be done elegantly). "Go on, have a look outside the door now," she said to me, before turning to chat with the other three.

Alone, I gently pushed the door open. And suddenly, I was leaning out of a caravan in a field of poppies swaying to a warm breath of breeze, facing a white-washed farmhouse with a backdrop of rolling hills. I could see, spanning across the hills, tiny dots of similar farmhouses, all surrounded by vineyards. The temperature difference hit me the second I stepped from the caravan. Spain – it had to be.

The others, unaware of my wonder as they chatted, melted from my mind as I felt the warmth of the sun. I had never seen Spain before, only pictures in my dad's National Geographic books. I couldn't help but swirl around in the field, arms outstretched, and face raised up to the cloudless sky, astonished at the way I was here, all at once in another country. Even after my dizziness from the spinning calmed, my mind still swirled.

I was reluctant to leave when I was called back to the caravan. Maria did the clicky thing and soon enough we were back outside Aunt Etty's.

I barely had a chance to remember where I was, before I was being dragged to a third caravan. This one had a snowstorm wrapped around its icy frontier, and perhaps it was just an optical illusion caused by its dazzling whiteness, but it seemed like the largest caravan. A woman with a gurgling baby strapped to her back was bent down over some washing as we appeared. She straightened when she saw us.

"Johanne," she yelled into the caravan's open door. "Your friends are here!"

A bright-eyed boy with almost white hair appeared in its frame. "You must be Emilie," he said, sticking out his hand for me to shake.

"Can you show her your home, Johanne?" Lori was asking him as we filtered into the caravan, having been waved inside by the lady. He too did the snaps and claps I was beginning to recognise, before handing around blue beanies as the caravan did the lurching action.

We huddled together for warmth as we stumbled out of the caravan, facing an unclouded lake, its colour matching that of the pure sky above, behind which white-headed mountains towered. The sky itself was a far cooler colour than the Spanish one. Majestic was the word it imprinted me with, and despite the biting wind, we stood there for a while, all five of us, staring into the lake as pieces of ice drifted across to blur our reflections. Despite the weather, I was even more reluctant to leave than last time. As we headed back to the caravan, no one said a word, and I thought about how wonderful it would be to stay here always.

"Not so wonderful as you may think," came Johanne's voice from behind me. *How did he know what I had been thinking?*

"June baby," he said aloud in reply to my unspoken question. "That's how I know."

CHAPTER SEVEN

Emilie

Alphie and I slept late the next day, waking up just in time for lunch. I spent the afternoon curled up on the armchair opposite the enormous (but sadly empty) fireplace. The rain had started again and however much I wanted to explore more caravans; I wasn't in the mood for getting soaked. I could feel a tingle of heat from my mug of hot chocolate, if not from the range, and I thought it was a shame that despite the rain, the weather was too mild to need the full throttle of the fire. As I sat there, I imagined it in the depths of winter, sending out its heat through all the corridors and passages of the house, raising up a magnificent orange face to beam out across the whole room. It would be so deliciously dramatic to be nestled in this armchair, novel in hand, warmed by the fire's magnitude, while the howling wind shook the glass panes and night's frost dusted the scene outside.

Alphie hadn't quite understood why I had wanted to come to the hearth for the afternoon – he takes the old thing for granted, having lived here so long. I could tell how peculiar he thought me when I asked Aunt Etty for the hot chocolate, scrunching up his face with a hint of disgust.

Alphie went up to his room after I had set myself up in the armchair. He told me to go and find him when I was finished doing whatever it was I was doing. He's lucky to have grown up with it all. I thought about how different my own life would have been if I'd grown up with my biological parents – if they had raised me as a Potensa, or at least given me to Aunt Etty instead of leaving me on the steps of some orphanage. I couldn't help but think of those little children we had seen out on the field yesterday – how happy they were to be playing with their powers. I wondered for a second why Aunt Etty hadn't adopted me too, as she had Alphie. She'd certainly kept tabs on me and had talked to my parents. I thought how incredible it would have been to have grown up here with Alphie. Then I stopped myself, realising that a life here would have meant a life without Mum and Dad and Lizzie. My breath caught in my throat and a wave of homesickness threatened to overwhelm me, not the first I'd had since I arrived. How silly Lizzie would have thought me, sitting there in front of a massive hearth and imagining a life I could never have known. I could just about picture her giggling as she rolled her eyes in exasperation.

Yes - I loved it here, but I loved it at home too. I decided I would ring my parents later on, just to hear their voices, just so that the familiarity of their tones could give me some comfort.

I was so occupied by these thoughts that I didn't notice the door opening, nor the person entering, until she stood right beside me. It was Aunt Etty, bedecked in a shawl now, and with a touch of tenderness that made her mouth curl upwards at the edges.

"Hello," I said, surprised at her appearance, trying to gather my thoughts and desperately willing myself to keep my voice steady and not cry at the thought of my family in London. "I was just day-dreaming, Aunt Etty."

"May I join you, my child?" she asked, not waiting for my response before placing herself carefully in the armchair adjacent to mine. I turned to sit myself upright. If I thought her intimidating when we first met, now that I knew who she truly was – the Head of the Potensa - she seemed all the more terrifying. Yet she had warmed to me somewhat: her tone was less sharp, her posture more relaxed. It looked as if she trusted me.

I wanted to ask if I could begin learning how to use my powers. It felt strange that I was full of unleashed potential, dozing inside me still. But somehow, I felt it wasn't my place to approach the subject. Luckily, she seemed to understand my feelings without me saying a word.

"I'm sure by now you are desperate to start your training," she began, in a commanding tone. "And that day will indeed come soon."

All homesickness left me and I practically squealed in excitement, before covering my mouth with my hand, realising I was too old for such a childish show of joy.

"But first," she continued, and here she looked down her nose at me, "there will be other lessons you need to learn. You haven't been able to grow up in the community and so we need to make sure that you will be able to handle your powers."

I slumped back down in my chair slightly, deflated by the news of yet more waiting.

"It's like learning a new language, I'm afraid. It only grows harder to master the older you get." Here she paused slightly and seemed to shoot me a warning dagger before continuing, as if to tell me that we were reaching a touchy subject. "But when the time is right, *Alphie* will be training with you too. I have gathered that you are aware of his slight … lack of progress … in this field. Over my many years I have learnt that everything happens for a reason, and often having two pupils is much more effective than one. Maybe that's where I've been going wrong with Alphie all this time."

"Oh I'm sure it's no-one's *fault*!" I spurted out, before realising how silly it sounded coming from me. "I'm sorry," I said, lowering my head slightly, "all I meant is that I'm sure Alphie and I will have great fun in our lessons."

"Fun is all well and good," Aunt Etty was saying, heaving herself up from the armchair, "but this is serious business." She began to make her way back to the door, having said what she intended to. But at the first creak of the hallway floorboard, I realised that there was something else I was desperate to ask her about. The question had been in the back of my head since Alphie had hinted at it yesterday.

"Oh, Aunt Etty," I called after her, causing her to turn around sharply. Seeing her face, questioning – and did I sense some impatience? – I hesitated and waited as it softened into a nod of encouragement.

"I need to know… about my parents," I said. Aunt Etty visibly drooped, suddenly looking even older than usual. "My *biological* parents."

Sighing, she came and stood before me once more. I tried to explain further, but she held up a hand to prevent me.

"Some things are too weighty to carry. Let me carry them alone for now, child. Just know that I loved your parents – I loved them both very much. But I can't bear to talk about them right now. Please, leave the subject here, my dear."

***

Emilie

I sat in silence as she left. It hurt so much – not knowing

anything about them. It hurt even more now that I knew what they were. Etty's use of the past tense had wiped away any secret hope I might have been nursing that they were still alive.

So, I sat there, dwelling on all I might have lost over the years, dreaming up what my parents might have looked like. How they might have loved me. How much I would have loved them.

After a while, I wandered into the kitchen, dragging my hands along the wooden panelling as I pulled my feet through the corridors. I felt like the same feeble, lonely child I'd been before being adopted. They were only vague memories: sensations and glimpsed pictures rather than moving images of solid colour. And I knew it was ridiculous. I'd never been so surrounded by love in my life, not only did I have my family and friends back in London, but I now also had a family in Aunt Etty and Alphie, and new friends in the twins too. But I supposed it was impossible to be rational all the time about matters such as love. Indeed (even after all my reminders about the wonderful people in my life), the feeling of distant neglect hung onto me like a parasite.

I drifted into the kitchen and sat down in a chair squarely facing the table in the centre of the room. Slamming my hands down in front of me onto the table's hard surface, I hung my head between my outstretched arms. I'd like to think I felt the weight of my past on my shoulders, but in all honesty, it was probably just the stiffness from all the running the day before. I breathed in and out, in and out, again and again, trying to ground myself and escape the illogical hauntings of neglect which were bearing down on me.

That's when I heard an awkward cough coming from the doorway. I wrenched my head upwards to see Alphie standing there. My cheeks flushed and my voice caught in my throat, but I managed to raise a pleasant smile to clear the tension in the air.

"I just came down for a glass of water," he said, and crossed over to the sink, clearly wondering whether to speak or to wait for me to talk.

"Alphie," I said, making up my mind as he turned back with a full glass, "what do you know about my parents?"

He sighed and hesitated, and then pulled up a chair opposite me at the table while folding his hands on its surface and deliberately taking his time as if to delay his response. When he finally spoke, it was full of pauses and breaks, his tone low, basically whispering.

"In all honesty, I don't know a great deal about your parents, Emilie. At least I don't know a great deal which is grounded in fact, but there is much hearsay I've encountered over the years." He paused.

"Please," I begged, eyes raised up in hope, "I just want to know something, anything, anything at all about them, and Aunt Etty told me not to ask her. She said it was too painful for her to talk about them."

"Alright then," was his reluctant reply, "but I swear I don't know much!"

I nodded eagerly, shoving his doubt into a hidden corner of my mind.

"Grandmother never likes anyone to discuss them, so it's not just with you that she's obscure. She used to have their photographs blazoned all around the house, their wedding pictures, photographs of your mother as a teenager – I think she was in control of light like you – Grandmother even had pictures of the two of them carrying out infantile absurdities together as children. They were childhood sweethearts, you know."

I didn't. Nor did I know what "infantile absurdities" were for that matter.

My lips puckered slowly as he spoke. I was busy imagining what it would have been like for them, for my real parents themselves, to run down these halls as children, their cries echoing through the corridors hollowed out by happiness.

"Then after they died, and Grandmother never told me how or why or where, she took all the photographs down, those of my parents included. I remember those images only vaguely myself; I was so young when it happened. It was Mrs Sanders who conveyed to me exactly how many photographs used to bedeck these halls. She mentioned it once, only in passing, but immediately closed up when I attempted to enquire further about the matter. No one has ever wanted to talk much about what transpired."

It burned me that their presence had been ignored for so many years. It simply wasn't fair that no one would tell me about my own parents. The injustice was acid in my throat.

"There's only one inkling I've ever been given about their demise. It was last year, when I stumbled across a box full of notes and a couple of articles. I couldn't make heads nor tails of it, and Mrs Sanders took it away from me when I tried to question her on it. But one article was flaunting a headline telling of the ten year anniversary of the 'Resurgence of the Evil'. It seems that then, or so I gathered from the article, several Potensa turned and abandoned the moral path. I know… I know that…"

Here he stopped completely, closing his eyes as if to consider whether or not to tell me what he was about to say. I pushed him to continue. Ignoring the fact that I didn't even know what the Resurgence of Evil was.

"I know that the resurgence, the one from ten years ago, caused the deaths of several of the most noble Potensa, including my own parents."

"So, it could have been then that they died too – my parents I mean." I finished his thought for him. "It could have been then that they were… killed. For their moral stance. Their goodness." *They must have been so wonderfully good.*

I felt the air around me bear down, about to swallow me, and I almost wished it would. *What was the Resurgence of Evil? Who had killed my parents?* But for some reason these thoughts couldn't form coherent sentences; I ran upstairs, head clouded. As I reached my bedroom door, the pent up tears finally began to stream, and I couldn't even make it inside before I collapsed on the floor.

***

Azariah

I saw Emilie rush upstairs, wishing desperately that I could be there to bring her some comfort. But with only the power of sight, I was useless at that moment, not that there was much comfort to give. That article had not given the full story. Alphie knew even less than he thought he did. She lay wrecked on the circular landing, the very picture of desolation. I just wished I could be a more active guardian, but Etty had forbidden that for the time being. But now Emilie had been told about the Resurgence of the Evil I feared all the more strongly for her.

Let me explain a little more about the Resurgence for you. The original Evil began when Ordinaries started to kill Potensa in an attempt to steal their powers. It was all eventually calmed down, as Etty had earlier explained to Emilie, and the Potensa entered the shadows. However, resurgences occurred. One particularly devastating one was put down by the aforementioned great great great great great great grandfather who had created the rooms. And ten years ago, Etty too had had to face a resurgence. Similarly, for me, the pain is still too real and raw for words, and peace holds only a tentative grasp. Over the past few years Potensa have started to disappear out of the blue once more, and for all Etty's control, fear still lurks in the background of many of our lives. But I shouldn't dwell on that, this is Emilie's story after all.

I saw Emilie look up sharply, face drawn with a red nose and swollen eyes, as she saw the little door to the landing open. She sniffed twice, wiped her running nose with the back of her arm, and muttered, "It's alright – I'm just here." It was Alphie, now rather embarrassed.

"I'm so sorry Emilie," he started, still bent over in the open doorway, "I should never have simply sprung that information on you. It was wrong of me – I knew it wasn't right, but I did it anyway and look how it turned out." Now his eyes were beginning to water too, as if Emilie's sobs were contagious. She began to smile, amazed that her own upset was mirrored in her cousin. She patted the bit of floor next to her, and Alphie shuffled up to sit close by, both of them resting their backs against the wall, knees drawn close to their chests.

"You didn't do anything wrong," she reassured him, looking deep into his eyes to confirm this fact. "It was just me reacting badly. I do that quite a lot." I was glad she could admit it.

She wiped her nose again with the back of her hand.

"It's not easy to hear that your parents were probably murdered," Alphie protested, but then his face twisted into another pained expression, thinking he shouldn't have raised the topic again. He always was a sensitive child, from what I had heard. I felt privileged to be there to see it first-hand. As a guardian, watching your young Potensa grow closer to others, gaining an insight into their personalities too – it's one of the best bits of the job.

Emilie breathed deeply and decided to adopt a maturity which might help them both. She softly laid one hand on top of his, giving it a gentle squeeze, and lifted up her eyes.

"Thank you for being honest with me. You're the only one who ever has. I really do appreciate it, Alphie. At least we're now in the same boat, what with the story of our parents' deaths being so alike." He gave her hand a gentle squeeze in return.

It was about ten minutes later that a loud gong was heard reverberating through the manor.

"That's dinner then!" said Alphie, jumping up. The pair hurried back down the stairs and into the kitchen. Though outwardly it seemed resolved, I could tell, that despite their deepening bond, the exchange weighed heavily on the both of them.

From then on, I watched Emilie intermittently. Most afternoons were spent with the twins down in the village or in the field of caravans. It fulfilled Emilie's ideals of the country lifestyle, and she was blissfully unaware of any cloud's looming shadow. I certainly sensed one, but it didn't take a shape I could recognise, and I didn't want to scare anyone with likely needless fears. Nonetheless, the feeling of unease lingered. For the while, I kept my tender eye on her, as is my job, relishing in her youthful love of life, and the kind of fearlessness that comes with innocence.

PART TWO
TRAINING

CHAPTER EIGHT

Emilie

*D*ays passed in a blur of excitement, exploration, and discovery. I felt like I had that one Christmas, many years ago, when I was given the *Sleeping Beauty* movie and watched it over and over again. Who knows, maybe Maleficent was actually a Potensa too? I had tired of it eventually, long after my parents had started regretting the purchase. But I knew I would never tire of this. Yes, I missed my family back in London, but there was something unmistakably alive about this place. It was as if even the grass in the meadow felt softer, grew higher, and constantly gave off the glorious odour of freshly mown lawns.

Mum said she could hear it in my voice when I phoned home: my excitement, my joy. She admitted everything to me once she knew I had been told about the Potensa.

"We always told you that you were special," she had teased. I had never heard her quite this animated before, quite this emotional. "Just not how special! Etty told us not to tell you until you started showing signs of powers yourself. That's why we've kept it a secret all these years. But do you remember a few months ago when all the bulbs kept blowing in your bedroom every time you had a bad dream? That's when we knew we'd have to tell you soon. Oh Emilie, I wish we could be there with you but Etty knows best. And now our very own daughter is to learn all about Potensa magic!

"But how do you know? Did Etty tell you? Does Lizzie know?" Questions spurted down the phone line, making my mum laugh.

"Yes, Etty came to us as soon as we said we agreed to adopt you. She explained the situation surrounding you, and a little of who the Potensa are. We couldn't quite believe it, myself even more so than your father, but I guess it is true after all, considering you've seen it!"

She paused, hesitated, then almost whispered, "It is all true, sweetheart, isn't it? There's nothing… upsetting going on?" She seemed to have a fear in her throat that wobbled her voice down the receiver.

But I just giggled, reassuring her that everything was just as it should be, and my mum's tone changed back to its old bouncy self again.

"You'll have to explain everything to us when you

get back! But no, Lizzie doesn't know. Etty said it was best to keep the number of people who know about your biological parentage to a minimum. You'll have to tell Lizzie you were super bored over the whole long summer without her." Here Mum laughed again, and I couldn't quite tell whether she was joking or in earnest. I guessed a bit of both. I wasn't sure I could keep all this from Lizzie though, even if she would be the least likely of all to believe me. How good it felt to be right...

"Just know how proud we are of you, darling."

And I did know.

***

Emilie

As the days drew on, my desire to begin training started to snowball. I could tell Alphie was a little more reluctant, but even he wasn't immune to my enthusiasm.

I wanted to ask Alphie what he thought would be inside his Rhisa, and yet it seemed too personal a question, just as nobody had asked me what I had seen in my Rhisa. Had someone asked, I'm not sure I could have explained it anyway. It bothered me a little: my pull to the darkness, those whispers. Somehow, I couldn't shake the feeling that I wasn't supposed to feel a draw to both the light and the dark. Darkness must be evil right? The thought lingered in the back of my mind everywhere we went; I carried it around in my pocket. And it scared me, if I'm being completely honest. I considered going to Aunt Etty about it, but I didn't want her to think that I wasn't ready for training yet and put it off even longer. I could have asked Alphie or the twins I supposed, but I didn't want to dampen the fun we were having, and I didn't think they'd really know what to do anyway. Besides, I persuaded myself, darkness is just a natural balance to light.

Right?

***

Azariah

A week or so later, on a day when the sun dappled everything a slightly brighter shade than normal, I saw Alphie, Emilie, and the twins playing a game of catch in front of the manor, it being the only game they could all agree on.

The game soon became competitive, with the two girls battling the boys to catch the most throws, their shrieks raised in pitch and their efforts doubled. Zander threw a particularly difficult shot to his sister in an attempt to force her to drop it, but Lori caught it deftly. Emilie gave her an encouraging high five and the pair exchanged victorious smiles. Next Lori threw it to Alphie, sending it so far that he had to run for it. But he too demonstrated his fine coordination skills, despite tripping slightly as he caught his prize. The others watched in amusement as he rolled on the grass before tossing it back to Emilie, who prepared herself to challenge Zander to a difficult throw. She threw it hard, straight at him, and the group held their breath as he braced himself to catch. And then, out of the clear blue sky, just as Zander was about to grab it, a sudden flash of bright white light lit up their vision. Zander dropped the ball.

The group looked from one to the other, all frozen by the unexpected strike of what they assumed must have been the weather. They stood, silent, cautious, unsure what to do or say or even whether to continue or not.

I couldn't help but chuckle at their confusion. It's a reaction I've seen time and time again. Then Alphie, tension showing on his face, raised up a single finger, and pointed it at Emilie's left hand. It was clenched into a tight fist. Staring down, she too saw what Alphie had: it was glowing, only slightly, but still, definitely glowing. She gasped. Even I struggled to grasp all that was rushing through her head at that moment.

And then Etty was running out of the large front door. She was lolloping along in a rather ungainly manner, at least for a woman of her poise, clutching her shawl around her and screwing up her face into an expression that cried out 'anger'. Emilie shoved her glowing hand behind her back, and the others shrank back.

But Etty must have noticed their fear because she slowed down, relaxing her face and losing that angry look. She was still somewhat heaving and out of breath, as she reached them and stood silently before the girl, until Emilie plucked up the courage and pulled her still-glowing hand from behind her back.

"I see," was all Etty said. "Follow me please." And turning on her heels, she walked, now with renewed posture, back into the house, as Emilie scurried behind her, looking rather faint. Before going inside, Emilie turned once more to see the others' faces. She tried to give what she hoped was a reassuring smile, but her heart was pounding too much for it to be convincing. Etty sat her down at the kitchen table, in the same spot she had first told her about the Potensa: how fitting.

But this time it was Emilie who had to do the talking.

"Tell me," Etty started, "what did it feel like?"

I could practically see Emilie's thoughts whizzing around inside her brain as she held up her hand before her eyes to examine it. Although its glow had almost disappeared, there was still an intriguing yellow tinge to it. She felt it over, stretched it out, considered how it felt at the end of her arm.

"My mind went blank," she began. "That's why at first I hadn't even realised that the flash was because of me. It was as if I had fainted. Then Alphie pointed to my hand. It felt… heavy, I suppose. Like I had been lying on it for ages and lost all sensation, but then that changed to pins and needles. It's still tingling slightly. And I think I have a bit of a headache."

Etty listened intently as Emilie tried her best to

explain, giving her an encouraging nod to urge her to continue. Emilie took a deep breath to calm her fluttering heart and gather her thoughts. I could tell that she was trying her best to make her words as clear as possible.

"I think I was subconsciously trying to make Zander drop the ball," she said. "We were playing in teams and I guess my competitive spirit must have got the best of me." Here her tone changed, and excitement flooded through her words, her face alight with amazement. "I'm actually a Potensa, Aunt Etty! I mean, I know you said I was, but I couldn't believe I'd actually be able to *do* anything already, and it's quite hard to believe when everything is so frustratingly slow! But I can actually do it!

I could see that Etty was trying not to laugh as she attempted to follow this stream of eagerness, but she had things she needed to tell her great-niece.

"My child," she said, in a tone as calmed as Emilie's was frantic, "you have to be careful now. The first show of power is always the hardest. You must not get over-excited and lose control. Now that you've accessed your power you must learn to harness it."

"Does that mean..." Emilie jumped up off her chair to run around to Etty. "Does that mean I can begin my training?! Does that mean you'll begin to teach me now?!"

"It does indeed," came Etty's smiling response. Yet even she was taken aback when Emilie threw her arms around her shoulders, squeezing her tight while whispering 'thank yous' in her ear.

That is the one and only time I have ever had access to Etty through sight, although even then it was only for a split second.

Alphie had never been so quick to embrace, thinking that his grandmother wouldn't approve of his sensitivities. But I think that Emilie's hug softened her, because as she held back her great-niece to look at her, a tiny tear trickled down her wizened cheek. I knew that tear wasn't just for Emilie,

"You're going to be wonderful," Etty said, and I would like to think she surprised even herself at the tenderness of her tone.

***

Emilie

I could hardly sleep that night, knowing that the next day I would begin my training to become a proper Potensa. I wondered what Mum and Dad would think. Then I thought of my biological mother and father, and what they'd have made of all this too. How proud they too would have been of their daughter. I wondered what kind of powers they had – Alphie had said my mother's power had been light, but I wondered about my father's as well.

Eventually sleep did come, but it wasn't long before

I was awoken by the sound of Alphie crashing into my bedroom.

"Grandmother says that today's the day!" he announced, looking equal parts terrified and excited. He threw open my curtains, making me wince at the bright light.

"So, get up, clothe yourself, and then we shall rendezvous in the kitchen." And then he was gone. I was glad he seemed excited too.

Positively shaking, I pulled on my clothes, putting on my top backwards and tripping over my own feet while I rushed to shove on some socks. I hurtled down the stairs as I heard the gong sound, nearly losing my balance, and swung around the kitchen door to enter its warm glow, tinged by the smell of fried eggs. Aunt Etty was sitting with her hands clasped in front of her, and Alphie looked as if he were trying to mimic her level of composure, despite the air of nervous agitation about him which he couldn't quite hide. Aunt Etty motioned to a chair before her, and I sat myself down, also trying to calm my jitters and show that I was mature enough to start training.

"The key word for today," Aunt Etty began (I was pleased she was getting straight into it), "is caution. You must be very careful in everything that you do, and follow my instructions precisely at all times, without adding any flairs of your own. Do you understand?" She looked directly at me as she said this last bit, obviously knowing that I would be the one to try to add any 'flairs of my own'.

I nodded eagerly in agreement ready to accept any conditions and was disappointed when a plate of eggs was placed before me.

"Breakfast first," was Aunt Etty's command, and although the eggs stuck in my throat, I obeyed as best I could. It didn't take long for me to finish. The eggs also seemed to bring about a sudden change in Alphie who simply moved his food around the plate, and I remembered back to my first afternoon exploring the caravans, and Alphie's frustration at how he wasn't very good at being the "special one". Aunt Etty pretended not to notice and rose from the table to lead the way out.

I practically leapt up. Alphie and I trailed after her, whispering to each other in hushed tones. I could tell Alphie was nervous, but then again, so was I. Who knew what today would hold?

When we reached the Rhisa, Aunt Etty whipped around to stare down at us both sternly. "Please do stop that childish whispering. It is time for you both to be mature."

We hung our heads and tried to concentrate on the task ahead. Aunt Etty told us how she was trying a new approach, because apparently young Potensa rarely trained using the Rhisa – most being taught at home by their parents. The purpose of this new approach was to help me connect to my powers properly, but also to push Alphie out of his hesitations. He flushed slightly as Aunt Etty mentioned this, and my heart went out to him, imagining he was reliving his past failures to harness his power.

"You will each step into your Rhisa," Aunt said. "All I want you to do is to stand in the middle, close your eyes, and try to sense the power that is around you. Do not, under any circumstance, try to do anything with that power. Do you understand?"

We both nodded, moving to stand in front of our respective Rhisa. Aunt Etty pushed open the doors without a single flourish.

I stepped inside and the warm golden light immediately drew me inwards, pulsing within me just like before, blood heating my hands, energy steaming my veins. Looking down, I saw once again that my hands were glowing, this time more brightly: a flame compared to earlier sparks. I walked forwards in a trance, pulled by tiny golden tendrils gently coiling and swirling around my ankles.

"Close your eyes." came Aunt Etty's voice from outside the Rhisa. It seemed removed, as if she were calling from across a cavern, but I obeyed anyway, standing still and rocking slightly, feeling the light reach through my closed eyelids. The tendrils began to rock me from side to side, hushing me into an even deeper trance as the light grew stronger inside my mind, blocking out all other thoughts. I was wiped clean as a slate and imprinted with nothing but strong white brightness. My hands began to tingle, just as they had after the lightning bolt, and I had that wonderful, beautiful feel of my power. I stood there and let it wash over me.

Then the whispers started again. Just like last time but now more coherent. With a chill, I realised what it was they were whispering. *My name.* They were whispering my name. I began to sense the darkness again, watching me, creeping up on me, reaching out to touch me, just as the whispers were. And the darkness too had tendrils, wrapping and tangling around me, trying to force back the light. My hands began to shake uncontrollably, like I was losing power over my own limbs. I strained to keep them still, to feel only tingles instead of shakes, but soon they were vibrating with a power that panicked me. I started to breathe heavily, trying to think only of the light, to focus on it and let it fill me as it had just a few seconds ago. But now the dark tendrils were fastened tight around my feet. I tried to move towards the light but couldn't, I tried to walk backwards towards the door, but I was stuck to the ground. And so, I just stood there. I knew I should fight back harder; I knew that's what a true hero should do, and I wanted to be that hero. *But it was so much effort.* It was as if the darkness had invaded me and muddied my senses, made any reasonable strain of thought impossible. It was telling me to give in, showing me how pointless it was to fight. But what terrified me most was that I wanted to listen, wanted to give in. What use was fighting when my feet were trapped and firmly held down. I could feel the tendrils reaching up my shins now. Eager. Hungry.

Then I remembered Aunt Etty's words of caution, Alphie's story of my parents' deaths during the Resurgence of Evil. Darkness was evil, right? I didn't want to be evil, didn't want to condone my parents' murder. I wanted to be a hero, the classic kind like the prince in *Sleeping Beauty*, who fights through brambles and dragons to do what is right. That must have hurt. Fighting dragons took effort, brambles scratched. But still he fought. That was what mattered. That was what I had to do. I heard a hiss like water dropped on burning coals and felt a little more clarity in my head, like the darkness was being pushed out. Maybe that was what was hissing. Like a snake that knows its head has been crushed, but still fights on.

Strength returned and I thrashed around, feeling tears begin to fall down my cheeks. And as one dropped off my chin, I heard that hissing sound again from beneath me. Then another tear fell, making the same sound. My feet were becoming less constrained, as my tears burned the tendrils of darkness. It hurt. Unbearably. I wanted to cry out and fall down, but I knew I couldn't. Although I didn't dare to open my eyes, I kept reaching for the light in my mind. Kept crying.

And soon I could feel only the light once more.

I began to walk slowly backwards towards the door, not daring to move quickly, trying not to awake any sleeping beast that might be resting in this room. I felt the door behind me, and yanked it open to stumble back into the corridor.

Heaving in breathless release, I finally opened my eyes. Aunt Etty didn't seem worried about my appearance, merely stroking my shoulder to calm me. I tried to explain what had happened in throaty chokes, but she stopped me, saying that only a Potensa of my birth month would ever be able to understand what went on in my Rhisa. And so I was silenced, and decided not to tell anyone of what I had experienced. I just hoped that silence was the right decision to make.

CHAPTER NINE

Emilie

*O*ur time in the Rhisa was mentally and physically exhausting for both of us. Apparently, it had been only five minutes but it didn't feel like it. Time didn't seem to have power in the Rhisa.

Aunt Etty sat us both down with a cup of tea and a digestive. I'm not normally a fan of tea, but Aunt Etty heaped spoonfuls of sugar in, and its sweet-bitter strength proved exactly what I needed. Forbidding us from speaking to each other of what went on inside the Rhisa, Aunt Etty left us to our drinks while she went to "prepare the next task."

I was already less certain about this whole training thing. I had expected it to be more fun, and decidedly less tiring. But there was no backing out now. It was as if Alphie and I had switched personalities. Where before he had been nervous and I had been excited, now it was the other way round. We didn't speak exactly of what went on in each of our Rhisa, but Alphie couldn't contain his delight at his obvious success inside. I hadn't seen him so animated in a long time and it was marvellous to see his old chivalric flair again, but somehow it stung me.

"I've never felt my powers that vehemently before," he had whispered to me as we were coming down the stairs to the kitchen, "I sometimes even doubted if they were there at all and impugned Grandmother's assertions that they were." It was as if his confidence had made him all the more dictionary-spoken. "Why hadn't she given me access to that trove before today? It was exhilarating!"

I had smiled encouragingly at him, containing my own disappointment behind the upturned corners of my faking lips. I had never tried hiding my feelings before and I was surprised at the ease with which I was able to do it. But his joy made me feel even more concerned that what had happened inside my Rhisa wasn't what was supposed to happen at all.

But there wasn't much time for me to reflect on it. Aunt Etty reappeared in the kitchen and was leading us to our second task. She took us out to the drive, and placed us at two tables, set up at least six feet away from each other.

"I thought it best that this task take place outside," she explained to us, "just in case you lash out unexpectedly." Although her tone was calm, her words worried me.

I glanced over to Alphie at his table, who gave me a cheeky grin. His table had four items on it – an empty jar, a glass of water, some soil in a handkerchief, and a box of matches. Mine had only an old paraffin lamp. I went to touch it, but Aunt Etty jumped at me: "Not yet, my child."

"Alphie is going to go first," she began to explain, "as he has tried this particular training exercise before. I hope your time in your Rhisa will make your attempt today more profitable than last time."

I expected Alphie to blush at her criticism, as he had done so many times before, but instead he merely adopted a determined expression – brows furrowed, lip bitten, eyes narrowed. It seemed that silence was demanded for the moment, and so, saying nothing, I turned to watch him at his task.

He turned first to the glass of water, placing his hands around the cool edge and staring at it intently. He seemed to strain, his knuckles whitening. Taking a deep breath in, he exhaled through pursed lips, and a small groan escaped. As if connected to the groan, a small spiral of water rose up from the centre of its surface, whirling in a circle and almost reaching Alphie's nose. It grew as he continued to exhale, until he could take it no more, and inhaled, relaxing every tightened muscle in his body as the water dropped with a small splash back into the glass. I wanted to cheer, to congratulate my cousin, but Aunt Etty glared at me as a small whoop escaped my lips. But despite that, I noted a similar look of pleasure light her own face. And was that pride too?

She motioned for Alphie to continue. He repeated the same task with the soil, leading it into a spiral which wavered about in the breeze. As it collapsed back to the handkerchief, Alphie was out of breath and restless, his face reddened; I noticed a trickle of sweat fall from his flushed cheeks.

"Would you like to stop here?" Aunt Etty asked him, monotone, refusing to give away any advice with her words.

"I'll continue," wheezed Alphie, a smile lighting his exhausted face. "It's never worked so well before and I don't want to stop now." He switched his old charm back on. "A knight's duty is to persevere." Aunt Etty prized him with a chuckle and an approving nod.

When working with the empty jar he merely clasped his hands in his lap and concentrated on pushing it over. The jar tipped sideways as if nudged by an invisible force – not from the outside but from the inside – and I realised that Alphie was controlling the air inside the jar.

He had successfully controlled three out of the four elements. I was so proud of him that I felt my chest contract into spirals, not unlike from the ones he had created.

But when he raised the match up before his eyes, shooting daggers into its tip, no flame was urged to spark. He tried for a full three minutes, becoming breathless, before dropping the match to the table with despair.

"No matter, Alphie," Aunt Etty was saying, her voice tender. "You've worked well today, my dear. Rest now."

And Alphie did, collapsing back in his chair. I wished I could rush up and give him a hug. But now Etty was looking at me. I just hoped she was planning on giving me slightly more instructions than she had to Alphie.

"It's all in the mind," she said. "Concentrate on the feeling you had in your Rhisa. Channel that power into your hands, and then transfer that power from your hands to the light of the lamp."

It sounded simple enough. I inhaled deeply. *I can do this.*

"Turn on the lamp and leave it at a low light for now," Aunt Etty continued. "As this is your first lesson all I want you to do is to increase the strength of the light. Place your hands around the light once it's on."

I did as instructed, flicking the switch from behind and adjusting it to a dim glow, but panic was rising in my chest. Aunt Etty had told me to concentrate on the feeling I'd had in my Rhisa, but that feeling wasn't altogether pleasant. It had been more of a battle than a feeling, and it had been pretty painful. Was I supposed to channel the determination I had felt, the tears, the barely triumphing light?

My hands trembled as I held the lamp. Closing my eyes, I thought of the Rhisa, and tried to push the sensation of brightness into my hands. Nothing was happening. I could feel very little; my memory of the Rhisa was floating away from me.

I chased it around the inside of my mind, searching in all nooks and crannies of my memory for a hint of the power I had felt before. I was truly beginning to panic now. I could feel only my breath quickening and my heart beating inside my ears, drumming away that I couldn't do it. Drumming away that I was going to fail. That I was going to be thrown out. That Etty would never look at me with pride...

I was angry. Angry at myself for not being able to do it. Angry at Aunt Etty for expecting me to be able to. Angry at her for shutting down my questions about what went on inside my Rhisa. Even angry at Alphie for being so successful already.

And then I caught it. The anger. The anger inside my mind was boiling away into a ball of hot fire, a ball of bright *light*. I felt its power. It rocked around inside my mind until I grasped it, forcing it into my hands, thinking now only of the lamp. I opened my eyes to see my work.

The lamp was beginning to glow, brighter and brighter, its once-tiny flame now pushed out in all directions. *I was doing it*. I kept feeling the anger, kept pushing out the light, until I too breathed out all my gathered tensions and dropped my hands. The light was extinguished immediately. But I had done it!

Alphie let out a small hooray and Aunt Etty

applauded in approval. I was on top of the world, jumping up to hug Alphie and emitting a squeal that couldn't be helped. A flash of deep pride sparked through me. Even Alphie hadn't done it the first time around, it had taken him months, maybe even years before he could.

I vaguely wondered whether it was bad that I had used anger to light the lamp, but it had certainly worked, and Aunt Etty hadn't seemed to mind or notice. I also wondered whether I should at least tell her about it, but her look of approval stopped me. What she didn't know wouldn't hurt her, and besides, she'd just say what she had before – that only someone with my power would be able to understand.

So, I brushed my worries aside, basking in the pride of success, a wave that carried me through the rest of the day.

***

Azariah

I saw it. I saw the flash of anger in Emilie's eyes – the way that she used it to control her powers. I knew that Etty hadn't managed to catch it, not from where she was standing. So, it was up to me to decide what to do with it. I had once used that same fuel to strengthen my powers. It was a mistake. But I certainly didn't use it as a child.

The power of vision is an interesting one, or at least I've always found so. Most January babies end up being guardians for younger Potensa – it makes sense since we can keep the best eye over them. It was certainly the profession my parents wanted me to enter into. I don't mind any more – in fact I quite like the job now.

When I was younger, I wanted to be a firefighter. Stupid, I know – such an Ordinary profession! The problem was that I was too good at it. I did try for a while, back when I was in my early twenties, but I found what many Potensa had found before me. It's no use being a Potensa in an Ordinary profession. You have to quell your powers and others suffer the consequences. It leads to great frustration – I know that now. But I was young and stupid back then. We'd all be sitting around the table playing cards, on standby for the next emergency that came our way. I'd sense a fire nearby, see it using my powers, and jump up with a start. I'd want to rush immediately to the scene, but without the proof of an emergency call, my colleagues wouldn't believe me. So, I would sit there, agitated and useless, until the call came through. The others began to believe I was psychic, and I began to lose my patience. They became suspicious, and I had to disappear.

Anyway – back to Emilie. I do apologise for my diversion, I meant only to explain why Ordinaries and Potensa are best kept separated. And if Emilie were to lash out in a situation like that, if she were to continue to use anger to spur on her powers, then the results could be very disastrous indeed. I knew I needed to tell Etty, she would know what to do, but I didn't want to. I had no idea how I'd possibly do it, and it felt like a breach of trust somehow.

Still, if Emilie was in trouble then it was important that Etty knew so she could decide what to and how to help – something I'd never know. That's why she's the Head and I'm not.

She would never have wanted to be a firefighter when she was younger.

***

Emilie

Alphie was just as excited as I was, and having been released from training after lunch, we rushed down to the village in the afternoon to update the twins on our success. They were playing tag with the younger kids out on the street as we arrived but ran up to us as soon as we were spotted.

"So?" Lori was the first to ask, holding her breath in captured suspense.

"It worked!" declared Alphie. "For both of us! We reigned triumphant!" Lori squealed and threw her arms around me.

"I never doubted you," laughed Zander. "I mean – not after that flash on the field!"

We joined in with their game of tag for the rest of the

afternoon. The twins' joy was easily visible, especially towards Alphie. They kept on running up to pat him on the back or hug him – it must have been hard on them too I guess, continually watching him fail and put himself down for it.

Before too long, Mrs Sanders was calling us in for tea, insisting that Alphie and I joined them. And now that I had been told all there was to tell about the Potensa, the twins' horde of siblings suddenly came into themselves. The table was being laid as we entered, except there didn't seem to be anyone laying it. The plates were picking themselves up out of the cupboard, flying through the air across the room, and clanging down in various places. Idara sat in the corner reading a book and I wondered for a second whether she too had the power of telekinesis.

"Stand back," said Lori. "Last time I got in the way, a whole pile of plates smashed, and Mum blamed me."

That's when we heard Mrs Sanders' voice from behind us.

"Visi, I've told you not to lay the table like that!" she scolded. Across the room, the five-year-old materialised, plate in hand and head hung in shame, evidently the one behind the mysteriously floating crockery.

"Now you know where his nickname came from," explained Zander laughing. "He's inVISIble, if you get my drift."

But Mrs Sanders was already turning to her seven-year-old.

"Aretta dear, do you think you could try to heat up the plates for us?" she gently encouraged.

"Okay, Mum!" came her quick reply, and she jumped up from the floor to stand over the nearest plate. She scrunched her face up into the smallest possible ball of concentration, holding the plate and squeezing it slightly until I could see it glow a low red.

"Done!" she announced triumphantly, dropping it back in its place and moving on to the next one. But before I could marvel over her skills, I felt a tiny tug at my leg, and looked down to see the one-year-old, Alesha, pulling at my shoelace. From where she had touched, a tiny shoot began to grow from the damp bit at the end of my lace. It looked like some of the cress I used to grow with my family when I was younger.

"Oh no, Ally," Zander moaned, having caught sight of the tuft of green. He brushed off the shoot from my lace and whipped Alesha away from me. "I'm so sorry, Emilie, she has no control over where she makes plants grow yet! Talk about green fingers..."

"One time," Lori chuckled, "we came in to see her entire cot covered in leaves! It took us hours to get rid of them all!"

I laughed as I bent over Alesha to stroke her soft crest of hair. She gazed up at me, dark eyes widened. I couldn't help but wonder if I had grown up in a Potensa family like the Sanders, whether I too would have shown my powers from a young age.

"So, power over plants then?" I whispered to Alesha, as if she could fully understand me. "My mum would have loved to have that when she was struggling with her roses last year!" Fabian, who had entered as I was speaking, laughed and scooped up Alesha to put her in the highchair. I couldn't help but feel a pang of homesickness as I thought of my mum.

But then we had to sit down to eat, and Mrs Sanders had baked the most deliciously smelling dish, which I was informed was suya chicken wings and jollof rice.

"It's a big deal for Mum to make anything with meat," whispered Lori to me as we tucked in eagerly. "Her power is over animals and she just hates to have to cook them! She has to know that they died of natural causes, however ridiculous that sounds! Once we had a venison pie and one of us made the mistake of asking where the meat had come from. Turns out it had been roadkill." She grinned and returned to the food.

It did indeed sound ridiculous, but then again, *all* of this would have seemed utterly fantastical to me a month ago.

Halfway through the meal, Mr Sanders battered his way through the door, out of breath and full of apologies for his tardiness. Kissing all his children on the head in a quick row, he rounded the table, managing to accidentally kiss Alphie on the head too. The whole table burst out in laughter. Realising his mistake and gushing further apologies, he quickly washed his hands and sat down on the spare chair.

Mr Sanders reminded me of a bumblebee for some reason, and his smile reminded me of my own dad too. There were now eleven of us at the table if you included little Ally, and we were just as squashed as you'd imagine. But the chirp and chatter of the family more than made up for it.

"So, the twins tell me that today was your first day of training," Mrs Sanders turned to ask me halfway through the meal. "How did it go?" Her dimples smiled down the table at me.

"Pretty exciting stuff, huh?!" added her husband through a mouthful of peas.

A tinge of guilt came back to me as I remembered the anger I had felt earlier that day. I certainly couldn't tell a whole table of ten about it if I couldn't tell Aunt Etty.

"It felt amazing!" I bluffed, looking down at my plate to hide my poor acting.

"It felt like a prestigious embrace of the highest level," added Alphie in his grand old style. But his obvious joy only plunged me into further doubts. Why had Alphie used happiness to fuel his powers but I had been forced to use anger?

I spent the rest of the meal in silence, ruined by the reminder of my mistake. We thanked Mr and Mrs Sanders for their hospitality and went home quite quickly; Alphie could obviously tell that something wasn't quite right with me. It seemed the twins could as well – I noticed them giving Alphie questioning glances after I'd hugged them goodbye – which only made me feel all the worse.

I lay in bed that night unable to give into the relief that would have been sleep. The same thoughts kept buzzing around my mind, unsorted and inescapable and the darkness seemed to close around me as it had in the Rhisa earlier. I refused to turn off the lamp for fear of what the night might bring. The painted couple stared down at me from the wall opposite my bed, and I stared right back, once again mesmerised by their eyes – my thoughts, fears, strains, and anger of the day twirling in my mind. It must have been very late when I heard a gentle rapping at my door.

A soft, "Emilie, are you still awake?" alerted me to Alphie's presence on the other side.

Hesitantly, I crept out of bed and let him in, unsure whether I really wanted to talk. We perched carefully at the foot of my bed, neither of us wanting to speak first.

"I'm sorry about being so quiet earlier," I said to Alphie, after a sufficiently long period of silence. "I've just got something playing on my mind. I'll be fine though." *I hope.*

"I could tell," said Alphie, shuffling an inch closer to me. "I was worried about you – I knew something was up. I figured that if I couldn't sleep because I was too busy worrying about you, then you probably couldn't sleep because you'd be too busy worrying about whatever this thing is which is making me worry about you!"

The confusion of his sentence made us both smile,

and I decided I would tell him what was on my mind. He probably deserved a little honesty. I inhaled, preparing how I was going to put it very carefully.

"So, when I used my powers earlier today," I began, slowly, "it wasn't joy or eagerness which helped me find them and harness them. It was anger." I paused to examine his face for signs of concern or fear or disgust. "I used anger to become powerful, Alphie!" I suddenly exploded, feeling a tear begin to trickle down my cheek, "And I know that can't be good!"

I bent over, feeling salty drops cascade onto my lap. There was a silence while Alphie considered what to say.

"I don't know that much about the ins and outs of magic either," he finally said, "but I agree that it doesn't sound exactly marvellous. We'll have to discover a way for you to use something other than anger to cultivate your powers."

He made it sound so simple. But then again, I had only used anger the one time. Perhaps there was still hope that I could learn to use another emotion to help me?

"Let's do it now." It was unusually direct for him. "No time like the present."

He hopped off the bed and turned on the main light. He twisted the dimmer on the light switch just slightly so that the bulb glowed a gentle amber. I lay back on my bed, clenched my hands into fists on either side of me, and stared up at the light above me. I thought of my

Rhisa, but this time blocked out all thought of the darkness while I did so.

"I will not get frustrated," I said aloud, tones crystal and commanding. "I will not get angry."

"Think of your family," Alphie said. "Think of summer days, of downy pups, of sunshine – all those jolly mementos."

I laughed at 'jolly mementos'. And that laughter created a ball of light in my mind. It was brighter this time, and much more, well, bouncy. It was working. And the thought of it working made me so happy that I was able to push it into my hands. And then from my tingling hands, I concentrated on the light above my head. The change was small, certainly, but it definitely began to grow a bit brighter.

But then a new thought tunnelled into my mind. And suddenly it began to irritate me that my powers weren't working as well as last time, to irritate me that the anger had shown more success. My hands began to vibrate with frustration and then – pop. The light bulb had blown.

"So that was anger at the end then?" Alphie asked after a second or two had passed. I nodded silently, sitting back up and feeling wretched all over again. "Well, at least you found some success with the happiness first," he said gently, trying to reassure me.

It was true. I had improved. Now I just had to continue to ignore the anger and the darkness and to use only joy instead. But I had scared myself.

CHAPTER TEN

Azariah

I watched Emilie as she continued to train. Etty used the same exercise every day for a week. And every day for a week I watched Emilie sit outside with a lamp and try to block out the anger but make the lamp glow anyway. Some days it worked. Some days less so. I could see Etty's confusion at the rather random nature of Emilie's improvement, but after seeing Emilie and Alphie working together last night, I didn't feel the same need to tell Etty what was going on. At least, I didn't feel the need so desperately. I could sense Emilie's frustration at the training, and I was getting better at picking up on Alphie's as well. But I was hoping it was something the two of them could work out together. Perhaps there was no need to concern Etty at all. Emilie was certainly improving, and I didn't really want to get in the way of her progress. And so, for the time being, I stayed silent.

***

Emilie

I was definitely improving. After a week of the same exercise, Alphie and I came outside for training to find our tables empty. Swapping confused glances, we sat and waited for Aunt Etty's instructions.

We had barely sat down when she emerged in the doorway carrying a set of eye goggles. "Just for extra precaution!" she called as she walked towards us. Alphie may have looked nervous, but I couldn't help but chuckle softly to myself. The thought of either of us inflicting serious enough damage to need protective masks was ridiculous.

"Today we are moving on," she announced. "Today we are stepping up a level, children."

She made it sound like a game.

"Level One complete," I mouthed to Alphie and drew a big tick in the air.

"Level Two initiated," he mouthed back, as he pretended to push imaginary buttons. Aunt Etty continued unphased.

"Today you are going to use your powers without the aid of props. I want each of you to find a source for your powers simply from your surroundings. Emilie, you will go first. I want you to create a ball of light in your hands.

It's a sunny day, so that should give you a boost."

I was ready; I felt prepared. We all put on the goggles, and I began to concentrate on the job ahead. I didn't know exactly what would work, but I knew what I could try. I held my hands cupped in front of me and tried to feel the sun beating down on my open palms. I stood there for at least a minute or two, suspended in concentration. After a while, my palms began to sweat, and slide up and down a little against each other. Closing my eyes, I conjured up all the happiness I could think of and focussed my mind on the heat of the sun's rays, the sensation of the beads of sweat, and the light that was visible even through my closed eyelids. I found it again, like I had before – that ball of light tossing and turning around the inside of my mind. It rolled and grew; I relished in the power.

Then I heard Alphie squeal, and at the same time a flash went off inside my mind, almost like the one from the very first time I'd used my power. I dropped my hands in shock.

"Alphie!" barked Aunt Etty's berating tones as I opened my eyes. "How dare you put her off! Control yourself!"

I turned to see him hang his head in shame, and I felt it echoed in my own chest.

"I'm sorry I couldn't do it, Aunt Etty," I mumbled, refusing to look her in the eye.

"If you couldn't do it, then what was that enormous flash, you silly girl?!" she teased. And that's when I realised that the flash hadn't been inside my mind. I was amazed at myself – proud even. And I hadn't even used anger.

Smiling, Aunt Etty turned to Alphie. I could tell he was already cowed by his telling off, but he closed his eyes tight, and held out his hands, in the same way that I had. He stood there for at least five minutes; I had no idea which element he was trying to conjure. Finally, he held his hands up, half triumphant, half ashamed. They were wet.

"Water harvested from the moisture in the air," Aunt Etty said. "Not bad, Alphie. Onto the next one now – air should be easy."

It turned out that she was right, for Alphie simply had to blow and a breeze picked up. I was mightily impressed, but Aunt Etty betrayed no emotion. I knew that Alphie was supposed to be special, that he was supposed to have an advantage for having all four elements under his control, but she could at least have rewarded his small success with a smile.

It seemed like his strength was wavering now. He bent down to dig a small hole in the grass, and held his hands above the hole, one on top of the other. A tiny spiral of earth was drawn out to reach his hands. I started to applaud, but paused mid-clap when I saw Aunt Etty's face.

"That hardly counts, Alphie," she reproached him. "You won't always be able to have the earth directly beneath your feet."

I saw his eyes harden as he stood back up and composed himself for the final element. Fire. He hadn't even been able to conjure it when he had a match, so I didn't know how he was planning to attempt it now. He clasped his hands together, and squeezed them until his face went red. Nothing happened.

"I'm sorry, Grandmother," he finally said, his hands dropping. "I just can't do it."

"Training is over for today," she announced, turning on her heel and walking back towards the house. I looked at her with, for the first time, a mild hint of disgust, and ran to console Alphie. He was trying not to cry, and I wrapped my arms around him. I just wished I understood why Aunt Etty acted in that way.

CHAPTER ELEVEN

Azariah

$\mathcal{I}$ knew why Etty was being so tough on her grandson, but that didn't make it any easier to watch. He has so much to live up to, more than Emilie could ever realise.

And although I didn't tell Etty exactly what was happening with Emilie and what she was fighting with, I still decided that it would be good for her if she met Benny. I proposed the idea to Etty, and she seemed happy enough to arrange it. I kept secret the other reason why I wanted Emilie to meet him, especially since it's not really allowed. That's because I look after Benny, you see. He's my half-brother. So, a meeting with him would inevitably lead to a meeting with me.

Guardians aren't really supposed to meet their Potensa wards until they're adults. It's not a hard-set rule though, just a recommendation. Children aren't supposed to know about the guardian system you see – we don't want them to feel like they're being watched. Yet I've been so desperate to meet Emilie recently, so desperate to see if she's any different in person than from afar. I decided that this would be the best compromise all round.

Etty told Alphie and Emilie that they were going to visit a friend of hers – a friend who was rather injured and frail but had some important tales to tell them – Benny. I could tell that they thought the excursion slightly unusual, I could sense a question forming in Emilie's mind, but she didn't dare to ask it. I think Emilie might have been slightly disheartened by Etty recently, for she had seemed somewhat distant from her every time I checked in.

The day arrived when Alphie and Emilie were due to visit. I set out an afternoon tea for them – finger sandwiches, scones, jam, cream – and spruced up the house so it didn't seem too faded. I live in the village as well – the only Potensa family there except for the Sanders. We tend to keep under the radar.

Benny and I share a father, a proud one who lived to the mellowed age of eighty before leaving us. My mother lives in Cumbria, and Benny lost his in the Resurgence of Evil, just over a decade ago. Benny and I have always muddled along. My work as a guardian keeps us going.

I was illogically flustered when the doorbell rang. I

smoothed down my hair in the hallway mirror, before berating myself for being so vain when Emilie wouldn't even know who I was. I swung open the front door, and there the three of them stood. Etty was behind, beaming benevolently at me, while Emilie had a polite yet distant expression plastered on her face and Alphie was looking at his shoes. I welcomed them all in, but Etty insisted that she had errands to run and couldn't be detained. She said that Alphie and Emilie could make their own way back – and were to be back before dark, she warned them sternly.

I wondered what they must have made of me. It was strange not to know what Emilie was thinking, but it's too difficult to use my power and maintain a conversation with her at the same time. I tried to be as smile-stuck and open as possible, merely hoping I didn't come across as too peculiar. Neither said much. I told them to sit down at the table while I went to fetch Benny.

Before I left the room, I turned around to sneak one more look at Emilie. She and Alphie had their heads bent in whispers and seemed to be sniggering at various things around the room. Emilie was pointing at something on the wall. I glanced around the space, suddenly seeing our house through their eyes. The tired 1960s wallpaper was peeling in the corners, the landscape paintings were clustered and ungainly, and my attempts to make the house cosy with rugs and patterned throws instead made it claustrophobic. We were outdated. I suddenly felt foolish before these two young Potensa – their futures as yet uncharted, their potential as yet unachieved. I sighed, forced myself to look away, not daring to engage my powers. I went to fetch Benny.

***

Emilie

Benny's carer, who had welcomed us in, seemed a bit on edge. Perfectly lovely, the ideal host, yet agitated in some way. Alphie and I were certainly nervous. I'd never seen a house quite like this before – antique in the most charming of ways. There were a million and one things to look at on every inch of the walls and Alphie and I began chattering and pointing out different things to each as soon as we were alone. I partially wished that Aunt Etty hadn't left us here without her, but I was intrigued by this Benny we were to meet – along with his supposed tales…

***

Azariah

I straightened out Benny's collar before I brought him inside. I kept seeing him through the eyes of a stranger. How clunky his wheelchair must seem, how ungainly the burn marks on his left cheek, how intriguing his lack of a left leg, how unnerving the dullness of his eyes. His mumbling, lack of attention, sudden outbursts: strange, unexpected.

"The children are here, Benny," I told him gently. "The ones who want to hear about your experiences." He nodded solemnly, and I wheeled him inside and to the table. The entire time I couldn't take my eyes off Emilie's face, searching for shifting features which might show her emotions. I get somewhat lazy at reading real facial expressions thanks to my power. But there was nothing unusual as far as I could tell – she simply smiled politely and introduced herself.

We began to work on the sandwiches, and as we did, an awkward silence settled in the air. I asked the children about their day, but since there was little I didn't already know, I found it difficult to craft a full conversation from their replies. And since I couldn't tell them much about myself, that topic was a non-starter as well. Alphie chatted happily in his extravagant way but it was still quite a relief when the tea was finished, and we could get down to the reason they were here.

"Benny," I prompted, judging the time to be right, "why don't you tell the children about your life?" He didn't hear me at first – off in his own world, pushing cakes into his mouth without really registering what he was doing. I saw Alphie and Emilie switch their gaze to stare at him, making me feel embarrassed on his behalf. I repeated my question, this time tapping him on the shoulder gently to bring him back to the here and now.

So intense was his trance that he was startled by my contact and he jumped and started to choke on his mouthful of cake. I started banging him on the back, sending the children apologetic glances. They seemed to be taking it all in good stead though, barely changing their polite expressions throughout the raucous.

Eventually Benny had regained his composure but had forgotten what my question was. I repeated it for the third, and I hoped, the final time, making eye contact to ensure he understood what I was asking.

"Oh yes," he said gruffly, in his old croaky tones, for his voice was never practised enough to be smoothened. "I was young once, children, not as long ago as it may seem." I think it was the first time he had spoken all day.

But right from that start, I could tell that he was fully here for this moment, master storyteller as ever. "And I was full of ambition. A powerful force but also a dangerous one. Or at the very least, it was dangerous in me."

Knowing Emilie, I thought she must have liked the dramatic flair of his narrative.

"I was a hopeful youth, and I thought that the Potensa could change the world. Indeed, I still do, but in a different way." I could see the children's faces striving to understand what he meant. "I used to think that our powers were being wasted, that our potential was being quashed. Don't ever develop that vanity, children."

I searched Emilie's face. She was evidently

enraptured by Benny's tale, resting her chin on her hand to lean in closer to his tale. I could have been making it up, but I think there was a glint in her eye which suggested that she understood Benny's point. That she related to the emotions he was describing. It was promising, certainly, but it was also dangerous. For her to understand how he once felt – that was all the more reason for her to be listening to his tale.

"I was foolish," Benny was continuing, "and many years ago, when I was in school, I joined some other Potensa in forming a sort of secret club, along with my best friends Myra and Jonas who I had grown up with and thought of as siblings. We called ourselves social scientists, we saw ourselves as experimental radicals. I realised many years later that we were in fact nothing but bullies. Keeping our identities as Potensa hidden, we tried to manipulate the Ordinaries in our classes – see what we could make them do or say. We even scared a few teachers. Luckily for us, and I'm sorry to say not for lack of trying, no one ever got hurt. At least not physically. I shudder to think of the damage we inflicted in other ways."

Here he paused, and I could definitely read shock in the children faces, especially in Alphie's. He had clearly never encountered a malevolent use of powers, at least not personally. Emilie's response was harder to read, but, from so close, she would notice if I started engaging my powers to get inside her head. So, I left it for the time being.

"These ideas continued into adulthood," said Benny, "and I got in with the wrong sort. We decided to…"

Here he trailed off and glanced at me. He started fidgeting in his chair, wringing his hands, and looking heavenwards as if to hold back tears. I knew he'd probably be sweating, and I could sense his rising panic.

"You don't have to tell them everything," I whispered in a low voice. "Just try to finish the story." He nodded and tried to find his voice again.

"We decided to do some bad things," he said, his voice hoarse and sore. "I'm ashamed of what we had planned. I won't tell you the extent of our evil." He spat out the final word in a glob of self-disgust that landed on the table before him. We all stared at it for a second before he continued.

"Suffice to say that those who I thought were my friends betrayed me. But by betraying me they did the only good thing they've ever done for me." Here his tone grew in strength and he held his head up ever so slightly. "I'm glad they took my leg, and I'm glad they left me with scars. This way I'll never forget. This way I will always remember my shame."

He slumped down in the chair again, finally finished and exhausted from his tale. I made my excuses to the children and took him back to his room, praising him on a story well told and a job well done. I hoped our time out of the room would give the children a chance to reflect on his words. Besides, it may do you some good to think on them too. I warn you, do not forget about Benny.

***

Emilie

Did they know? Did they know about my tendency towards anger? The old man's tale had certainly startled Alphie and me. But Alphie's shock was full of fear of those who may have such hate within them – yet my fear was that it may dwell within me. I vowed to myself I would never make the same mistakes Benny did.

They came back down a little while later; Benny had recovered but now seemed rather lost and far away as if he was not really in the room with us. We had another pot of tea with his carer, and then thanked them for the afternoon. I truly meant it when I said I had learnt a lot. We left through the front door, breathing a sigh of relief as we left the heaviness of the house and its stories. The sun handed us its last rays and we walked under them in silence. I had a lot to think about. *Myra and Jonas*. Under my breath, the repetition of their names scorched my throat. What sort of people would betray and injure their own friend?

But something felt wrong as we walked back to the manor. The air felt somehow too dense, like it was bearing down on us. I could tell that Alphie felt it too. We were halfway back, far enough that the village was out of sight but not so far that we could see the house. As if urged by an unspoken word, we both sped up, not wanting to be left walking in the lingering, growing darkness. Etty had said before dark. That was okay. We could make it back by then.

We drew closer together as we continued, our feet scuffing in the light dirt of the track. And I, who wasn't scared of adventure, who wasn't scared of exploring old mansions at midnight, I was beginning to feel alarmed. I couldn't tell why – there was not something obviously scary around – and I'd often walked home in the evening back in London, but there was a feeling of dread, carried by the air, that filled my lungs with panic.

And as I was considering the sensation of foreboding that was pressing on my chest, a figure in a black jacket appeared on the road in front of us. I felt Alphie stiffen beside me. Slowly, I took hold of his arm and we continued, careful to avoid looking at the passer-by. And pass by he did, much to my relief. I felt a little stupid at having been scared by a random pedestrian but that feeling vanished a moment later as a second man appeared in front. The feeling of dread once again filled me and I strove to push it aside as we walked up to him, preparing to pass, looking again at the ground. Why was I so jittery?

As we drew near, the man stopped, standing right in the middle of the road. Fear rose up into my mouth, but I bit my tongue to stop it and slowly lifted my eyes. Alphie was trembling against me and I was about to encourage him to turn and walk back to the village when I heard it. Footsteps from behind. Closer now, drawing up on us. Turning to face the footsteps from behind, I saw the man we had just passed, black jacket somehow stark against the glowering, lowering light. I turned my head, looking for an escape to the side, but the bushes were too high for a mad dash. No witnesses, no-one watching.

Panic pulsed through me. We were trapped.

They lunged.

I tasted bile at the back of my throat and something that must have been a scream jerked from within me. My legs felt wobbly and it was all I could do to stand. Then I couldn't even do that. I fell. Saw black.

***

Azariah

I was putting away the last of the dishes when I heard it, ripping through the walls, reverberating. The sound of a girl's scream. Emilie's scream. I dropped the mug, barely registering the sound of breaking china. My power generally allows me to hear conversations as well as to see but in moments when someone lets down their guard and is overwhelmed by emotions, those sounds are amplified – for the mind turns into a cacophony of noises and thoughts and smells, all of which I have access to. I gained a brief glimpse of Emilie from above,

Alphie beside her, barred by two men, then by darkness. They had been attacked. That was the only explanation for my vision. The darkness meant that Emilie must have fallen unconscious. And no matter how hard I tried, I could not reach her. With a feeling of shipwrecked dread, I ran, dodging the broken shards of the mug, down the hallway and out the door.

My legs could not sustain the sprint I was attempting, and I was forced to slow to a jog. I reached the point in the road where I had seen the children attacked. Not a trace remained of either of them. Thoughts pounded against me. This was my fault. If only I had walked home with them, or at least kept an eye on Emilie as they walked, then I would have seen it all. I could have stopped it. *This is your fault.* The words kept rhythm with my feet, spurring me on.

The reason for Emilie's disappearance was clear. I knew only too well who would have taken her and the thought filled me with dread. Potensa had been going missing for years now, never to be seen or heard of again, but this was different. Etty had feared it from the beginning, had hidden things in the hope that it would protect Emilie. I tried to reach for her again, to see her, but I was once more met with darkness. Only Etty could help her now. I didn't have the heart to run any more. How was I going to break it to Etty, that I, Emilie's guardian, had failed – *and* that her grandson had been taken too. My steps felt heavy, like my heart.

It was with great effort that I was able to pull open

the huge double doors of the house. I heard Etty's voice from around the corner.

"There you two are, you're late."

My heart hit the floor.

"Well don't just stand there, come-"

She stopped as she rounded the corner, shock twisting her face. And was that fear, mirroring my own? No, Etty was never afraid.

"You'd better come in and explain what happened."

She didn't say it harshly, she didn't say it condemningly, but still I cringed under the weight of the words. Yes, I had better explain. I only hoped there was something she could do.

PART THREE
THE OTHER MANOR

CHAPTER TWELVE

Emilie

$\mathcal{I}$ woke, gradually pulled from the moment of intangible dreams to the knowledge that I was once again in reality. Keeping my eyes closed, I held on to the lingering whispers of my dreams as they slipped through into nothingness. Thoughts were slowly forming in my mind, memories and glimpses and a black jacket. I jerked up. Fully awake, the extent of my reality washed over me again in a wrench of panic.

Darkness – I could see nothing. I had the feeling of being in a gaping space. The thought engulfed me. I hated the feeling that I couldn't sense an end to the space, couldn't sense any walls around me. The thought that anything could be within the same space as me and that I would have no way of getting help only made my fear grow.

I took a deep breath to calm myself and slowly my eyes adjusted to the dark and I rose from where I lay, jerking my feet back as they unexpectedly met plush carpet. Disorientated, I rushed to where I hoped I would find a wall. My hands slammed into uneven rock. I breathed in sharply against the pain, panic once again welling in me. I hammered against the rock until I thought my fists would bleed, I shoved and shoved, before collapsing into the carpet. The rock was solid. Trapping me in.

Trapping *us* in, I thought in selfish relief. Alphie was here too. I could hear his heavy breathing in the dark and, as my eyes adjusted further, I saw him half a metre away in a similar bed to the one I had just left, curled up in sleep. Seeing his peaceful form calmed me and as my breaths slowed, my thoughts gathered.

Looking upwards I could see a lighter, deeper, more purple kind of black which I took to be a skylight. And at its centre, one tiny pinprick of light. A star.

Even here, wherever *here* was, light remained. And wasn't light my power? Reassured, I lay back onto the bed.

How kind of our captors to give us bedding. The thought made me smile and the smile made me feel powerful. I would not be cowed. Whoever had put us here would not break us. If that star could still shine, if I could still smile, they could never win. As I lay back down, I watched the sky through the skylight. I watched as the darkness lightened and turned to silver. Matching my breaths to Alphie's slow, deep, peaceful ones, I felt the lingering panic dissolve slightly.

I must have fallen asleep again because the next thing I registered was the deep reverberating clang of shaken metal and the growl of a man intending to wake us. It was lighter now, and a single spear of sunlight fell onto the middle of the floor. Through it I saw the man with the black jacket again, stomping back through a large metal door to wherever he had come from. And there was something else too. A table, with what looked to be a cloth on it. And the smell of toast. Through the light of the skylight, I was able to properly take in the place. It didn't seem as scary as it had before. A ruby rug softened the floor, a dresser hid the edges and curves of the walls, and two solid bed frames graced either side of the cavern. A mysterious, oddly beautiful cavern. And our prison.

Alphie was now awake beside me; I saw the same panic on his face that had been on mine when I first woke. He had a bruise on his jaw. I held out my hand to his as he registered everything, trying to calm him the way he had unknowingly done for me. In place of fear, I now felt anger. Anger for the bruise on Alphie's cheek, anger at myself for not having fought harder, anger at the people who had put us here.

Alphie stood tentatively and I followed suit. I could still sense the fear and confusion in him as we made our way to the table. It was small, low enough that we could sit on the floor, and the cloth covering it was

149

unnervingly white. Atop the table sat a stack of buttered toast.

"Do you think it's poisoned?" Alphie whispered, as if the very sound of the word might kill him.

"No," I replied with a sigh. "If they wanted us dead, they'd have done it already."

"Well then why are they feeding us?"

"I don't know," I lied.

But I did. I understood it perfectly. I didn't know why but I did know we were prisoners, welcome prisoners, and our host intended to keep us. I shivered. Whoever these people were or whatever they wanted, maybe a ransom, the food showed me that they had a purpose for us. One that I wasn't sure I wanted to discover.

***

Azariah

Etty listened with patience to my story as I gasped it out. When I had finished, I paused, feeling myself shake in the silence.

"Do you think it's *them*?" I asked after a moment, immediately terrified of the answer.

"Yes, I do," came the sickening reply.

"Well then we've got to get her out as quick as possible. She can't stay there. Who knows what they'll do to her?" My words seemed to be falling from me, trying to keep up with my rising dread. Etty nodded slowly. Her silence exasperated me. We needed to do something and do something now.

"Well?" I questioned impatiently. "What do we do? How do we rescue Emilie and Alphie?"

"First, we have to find *them*," she said. "When *they* escaped and evaded us last time, they made a point of hiding themselves. As people celebrated our 'victory', I knew better."

I nodded. I too had not felt secure in the jubilation of a decade ago.

"I knew they were waiting for the right moment, and it seems they believe that this is it. And indeed, it does seem like it. Alphie and Emilie have barely trained, they're only children. They'll be clay in their hands."

"But surely there must be something we can do?" I interjected. "You must have some idea of where they are?"

"I may. I have been stewing on it for years, collecting clues, but to very little avail. But, despite that, we must try."

"Of course we must try," I practically shouted. "And I suggest we leave immediately," I added, amending my tone.

"Yes, I think you're right." A pause.

"Benny!" I exclaimed, thinking aloud, suddenly remembering how in my flight I had left him alone.

"I'll send a message to the village; Mrs Sanders will look after him."

I nodded. There was nothing more to say. I prayed

with all my might that we would get to the children in time, that they would be safe, that they would stick to what they knew to be right.

And if you knew who these people were, you'd be praying the same thing.

***

Emilie

Once enough time had passed after eating to persuade Alphie that the food was not poisoned, his talk turned to how we were going to escape. He came up with a number of ideas, all of which were flawed, and uncharacteristically adventurous for him. But his fear was obvious, and it did strike me as strange that apart from the mad slamming in the midst of my panic, I had not thought seriously of escaping. The door was very clearly locked, the guard had made a point of demonstrating that to us as he left, and so I guess I had resigned myself to the knowledge that we were stuck here, and we didn't even know where *here* was. Alphie refused to acknowledge this, his fear increasing as the number of his escape ideas dwindled.

If I'm honest, a part of me was curious. Curious about who our captors were, what they wanted. Of course, I knew it couldn't be anything good, but the not knowing was almost worse. It was the same curiosity which had compelled me to explore the forbidden floor and to enter the Rhisa of light for the first time, and if I'm honest, I guess it was the curiosity which had led me to the darkness as well. I had wanted to know what it felt like, just as I had felt the light. Alphie just wasn't one to understand that, so I resigned myself to his panicked jabbering.

All of a sudden, he stopped talking. I hadn't really been listening but the silence now sparked my attention. I could see a man entering the cavern through the metal door, shutting it firmly behind him, ruining yet another of Alphie's desperate escape plans. It was not the man with the jacket this time, but the other one. I half expected him to have a scar running down the course of his face - the typical villain look. But he took a few steps closer until he stood right under the skylight, and as the light from above shone down on his face he suddenly didn't appear so intimidating. Why? Because he was handsome. I was ashamed at myself for the thought but his features could only be described as positively dashing – hair slicked back, teeth white and bright, eyes dark and deep. It felt completely wrong.

"I've come to take you to see the bosses." Despite his looks, his voice still grated like a rusty lock on my ears. Not that we needed any more locks in our cage, a key would be more useful. I smiled again at my own sense of humour. I was coping quite well under pressure. Alphie and I both stood, trying to make ourselves seem as defiant as possible.

"Just her. Boy – you're staying here." Confusion

briefly flickered across my face. Alphie continued to stand and looked directly at the man barely a metre away; I admired his courage.

"Firstly, I am not just some little boy." There was a slight tremble to Alphie's voice. "Either we both go or neither of us go." I could tell his directness was an attempt to sound strong.

The man laughed; the sound reverberated cruelly around the cavern.

"I don't think you're in the position of bargaining, *boy*. Either she comes without a fuss and you remain conscious, or I knock you out and then she comes."

I could tell he wasn't joking, despite the smile plastered on his face.

"What do you think? Want a matching bruise on the other side?"

Alphie looked like he was about to retort, but I put out a hand and stopped him.

"I'll come without a fuss," I said in the meekest manner I could muster, though anger pulsed at the thought of him hitting Alphie again.

"I thought you would. Good girl." I shuddered, feeling very much like the little girl he wanted to reduce me to.

He unlocked the door; I exited, and then he locked it again, leaving Alphie behind. Just before the door closed, I turned to see Alphie, hands on his head, looking the very picture of defeat. The guard grabbed my arm and I shuddered. My anger left me, leaving only fear in its place. We were heading for the bosses. What kind of people would kidnap two children but keep them in a luxurious cavern; would threaten them with violence, but then feed them breakfast on a clothed table? And why was I the only one summoned?

Emilie

The guard led me through the cavern and then up a set of stairs cut from rock. Six stairs. I counted them in an attempt to ground myself in reality, refusing to let my imagination scare me. The stairs led to the middle of a dimly lit, overly carpeted corridor. I could feel its thick pile sink underfoot. Luxurious and old. Like Aunt Etty's manor, but not nearly as well loved. Cracks in the panelling of the wall expelled darkness, holding my eye as we turned to the right and walked along the corridor. It was long; I had plenty of time to imagine the many prisoners who must have walked this same walk over dozens of derelict decades. There were no doors leading from the corridor, just more and more increasingly dark wood.

But the corridor did eventually end, at a curved wooden door. Opening it, the guard stepped back.

"They want to see you alone."

The door opened to another six steps, which hid the top from view. Panic again grabbed my throat and I took back my previous thoughts: they were going to kill me, and there would be no witnesses, not even the guard.

But he must have sensed my fear, as he tensed his shoulders, ready to stop me should I run. Whoever, or whatever (that thought sent a shudder through me!) was up the steps, I had no choice but to meet them. Steeling my nerves, I pigeon-stepped through the door, careful not to trip over the wooden edge of the frame and started up the stairs. If I was going to die, at least I would die dignified and heroic. Nobody but me would ever know, but even that thought had a strange romantic comfort to it.

When I reached the top of the stairs, I couldn't help the nervous laugh that escaped me, only for it to echo through the mammoth space as if in mockery. It was a hall, around the same size as my primary school hall, but that was where the similarity ended. It was peculiar that the thought of school had even entered my head in the first place, but I suppose I felt as out of my depth and intimidated as I had on my first day of reception. The hall was framed by a colonnade, bathed in shadow, on the opposite side from where I emerged. The ceiling was so high that I couldn't see its top, it seemed to just fade away. To my left, at the end of the hall, were large double doors, like the ones at Aunt Etty's – equally immovable in appearance. And at the opposite end of the hall were three ornate chairs. It looked almost like a throne room, or a room trying very hard to be a throne room, and despite my fear, I found that I quite liked it.

My attention was diverted by a small cough. Scanning the room for who had made the noise, I was able to just about make out two figures in the shadows of the colonnade. The bosses.

"Hello Emilie. Is it too dark in here for you?" came a cool male voice.

A jolt of fear sparked through me again, but curiosity swiftly followed.

I walked towards the colonnade, determined that I wouldn't let nerves tremble my legs, determined that I should show them I was brave and that I was the wrong kind of person to kidnap, determined that I would get my answers and then get out of here, taking Alphie with me. But as they stepped out from the shadow, all that determination crumbled, replaced instead by shock. Whatever I had been expecting, it was not this. I was so disoriented that I was forced to stop as my legs threatened to give way. Walking towards me, in the flesh, not in brushstrokes, were the couple from the painting on my wall in Aunt Etty's manor.

The woman looked the same but her smile that had seemed so sincere in the painting now seemed fake, as if the rest of her face didn't really appreciate it being there. The man too had the same sturdy appearance as his painting. I had dwelt on their design for so long – and now seeing them before me I shivered. Cold. Their eyes were definitely cold.

Who were they? They must know Aunt Etty, otherwise why would she have a painting of them in her house? Maybe Aunt Etty had authorised our kidnapping, trying to test us or something. No, Etty was cold and unforgiving sometimes, but she wasn't cruel enough to kidnap us and keep us in a cell. *Right*? But then who were these people? What did they want?

The woman's false smile expanded at the sight of my shock and confusion. She tilted her head encouragingly.

"Ask your questions, we don't intend to harm you."

I was trying desperately to collect my thoughts, to change the twirling mass into understandable questions. Sights flashed through me: the painting, the black jacket, Alphie lying bruised on the floor, the star, breakfast, the panelled walls, this room, these people, the painting, Aunt Etty. None of it made sense. I almost wished I had stayed back in London – ignorance seemed like bliss. It seemed the more you know, the more you realise there is still to find out.

"You seem to recognise us," the woman prompted.

"Yes, yes," I began, the words tumbling out, "from the painting."

"Oh yes, the painting, I'm surprised Etty still has that."

"Why?" I blurted. "How do you know Aunt Etty? Who are you? Why am I here? What do you want with us? Where are we? And what *is* this place?"

The questions bubbled out of me, leaving no space for answers, yet begging for clarity. The woman laughed – a sweet sound. Too sweet.

"Which one do you want answered first?"

The answer took me aback. I hadn't expected her to be willing to answer the questions.

Which one did I want to know first? They all burned through me.

"Fine," I said. "How do you know my great aunt?"

"Ah, that's a big one," she replied thoughtfully. "Let's just say we have known her for many years, but we are no longer a part of her life. She cut us out, you see."

"Why would she do that?" I spluttered.

"She decided we weren't good enough for her," the man said gravely. It didn't exactly answer my first question, but I knew it would be useless to press further, and I had more to ask anyway.

"Well then, why am I here? What do you want with me and Alphie?"

"We wanted to rescue you," the woman said. "We know first-hand of Etty's deceit. And we need you."

"Need me?" That didn't make any sense. "What do you need me for? And my aunt is not deceitful!"

"We want to show the world who Etty really is. Life without Etty's strict rules has taught us much, there is so much that she keeps hidden, that she doesn't want us to have access to. We can finish your training. We can give you that power."

The moment when I had first unleashed my power spun to the front of my mind. I had felt strong, invincible almost. Since then, it had been harder to master it, frustrating even. Maybe Etty *was* deliberately making it harder.

"So why do you need me?" I whispered.

"We need your help to stop her. To tear down all that she has built and replace it with true freedom."

The man said it with such ease, as if it was the simplest thing in the world.

"And what if I don't want to help you?"

"Well, let's just say that's where Alphie comes in."

I shivered at their threat, hating to think of what they might do to him. There was no apparent cruelty in the man's voice, but the underlying danger was evident. None of it made sense.

"But why … why do you hate her so much?"

"You know, I used to call her 'Aunt' too," the woman replied bitingly, with an acidic laugh that didn't show on her face. "Etty was like a second mother to me. After my own mother died, she took me in, just like she took your cousin in. She taught me, she taught both of us." She gestured to the man beside her. "But then she decided that she didn't want us anymore, told us we weren't to be trusted, turned a whole group of Potensa against us and banished us. Us and all our friends. Simply because we didn't want to stick to her rules, because we wanted more for the Potensa race. We refused to leave without a fight, and it took an ugly turn. People got hurt – people died – Alphie's parents included. I guess she took him in because she felt bad for him. Guilty for causing their deaths." She paused for a moment, eyes trailing on the ground. "Meanwhile…

we were forced to leave our beautiful baby daughter on the steps of an orphanage."

She lifted her head and fixed her sad, cold eyes on me.

CHAPTER THIRTEEN

Emilie

M y mind reeled. I felt like the ground should be shaking, keeping time with the upheaving foundations of my world. My parents were alive. Standing right in front of me. I couldn't comprehend it. All these years they had been alive. My first thought was to run up to them, to hug them, to live out the daydream I had always imagined this moment would be.

But why had they taken so long to find me?

The thought glued me to the ground, stopped me from rushing towards them, held back joyous tears from my eyes. If these people were my parents, then my parents were the type of people who would kidnap children, who would lock them in caverns, who would threaten their friends. This wasn't at all how I imagined them to be.

Now the ground really did begin to shake, or maybe that was my legs. I fell forward and the man caught me. No, my *father* caught me. And his hands weren't half as cold as his eyes were.

"You should probably go back now. Alphie will be wondering why you've been so long, and we wouldn't want him to worry, would we?"

I think it was meant to be caring, but the memory of their threat against him only moments ago jarred me and I straightened.

"We're here for you when you're ready," my father said. "When you're ready to start training with us, ready to tear down Etty and her lies."

As if on cue, the guard entered to escort me back to the cavern. I had just reached the door when I suddenly remembered.

"Wait." I turned. "I don't even know your names!"

The man smiled. "I'm Jonas, and your mother is Myra."

The blood left my face. I stiffened. Jonas and Myra. Weren't they the people from the story Benny had told us only yesterday? The ones who had betrayed him?

I walked back to the cavern in silence, any hint of joy gone, more questions spinning around my head than when I had entered. More questions than ever before.

There was a rather immense part of me that wasn't sure I would ever lay eyes on Emilie again when she retreated from the cavern. Emilie had managed to persuade me that the food was not in fact poisoned, but the fact that the man had taken only her still rattled me. For all my chivalric jokes, I didn't especially want to die, not even to save a fair maiden such as Emilie, nor did I want to be left here alone. I decided to do the most logical thing and continue expanding upon my escape plan concepts.

Emilie had exposed fatal flaws in all the other ones – even when I was convinced they had been indubitably, undoubtedly fool proof. I was surprised at how adventurous I was being. I had suggested scaling the wall to hitch ourselves up to the skylight, and flee that way. Emilie had pointed out that the jump to the skylight would be too great and that there was nothing to grasp onto or to break the skylight with. I did agree that the furniture in this strangely decorated cavern would indeed be a rather impractical instrument for that particular purpose. The table or the dresser may have worked to break the glass, but the noise would have been far too risky. Besides, as Emilie pointed out, it wasn't the getting out that was the main problem – although even that seemed pretty monumental – but the getting home. Both of us had blacked out during the kidnapping and so neither of us had had our wits to track where we were being taken.

I resigned to think on the matter further. I didn't think I would be strong enough to make a tunnel under the door, but it was worth a try. I sat down, crossed my legs, and focussed on the stone tile below me. How on earth would I be able to move stone, if I could barely make a hole in the ground during training?

It took immense tenacity and stamina to push that thought away and even more to focus on the stone. I tried to bring to mind everything about the stone – its size, shape, colour, texture – and to picture it moving, picture it doing what I wanted it to do. But it was to no avail, it refused to move.

However, there was little else I could occupy myself with as I waited for Emilie to return. So, I continued. After a prolonged time where I honestly thought I might just about combust (although I wouldn't obviously because I still didn't know how to summon fire) I thought I felt the stone move the tiniest inch. But the amount of success it achieved for my escape plan was negligible – almost non-existent. I sat on the floor, trying to summon intermittent bursts of power, growing less and less certain, and more and more tired. Eventually I heard the resounding sound of footsteps outside the door, echoing in a way that only occurs in gaping, sepulchral caverns. I lay back, exhausted veins pumping exhausted blood. Maybe they'd come and take me too now.

But as tears veiled my eyes, the thought of resignation morphed into indignation.

No. I wasn't about to let them do that; I wasn't about to let them take me. If they came back and opened the cavern door, I would make a mad dash for it, find Emilie and escape. I knew that it was desperate and foolhardy, that I was thinking in a more 'Emilie' style, but it was better than sitting idly by and leaving my chance of survival to whoever grasped the reins of my fate.

But relief coursed through me as I caught sight of Emilie, led by the same man who had taken her, however long ago that was. I wished I had a watch on.

I could tell something was amiss with Emilie. She seemed dazed as she walked towards me, perturbed and muddled, as if even her very steps were zig-zagged. It looked like she was trying to figure out a complex maths problem or put together puzzle pieces that didn't quite connect. I had seen that look on her face when Etty first told her about the Potensa. All thoughts of a mad dash fled from me. I knew that I couldn't leave her, and I knew that in the state she was in, she wouldn't be able to respond with the agility needed for my escape plan. I sighed internally but tried to construct a smile. I had to save face for her.

But Emilie wasn't even looking at me. She was looking down at her fingertips as if something there could help her understand whatever it was which was perplexing her.

The guard unlocked the door, just long enough for Emilie to walk in, and then locked it again. I waited until he had left the cavern before turning to her.

"What happened?"

She looked up at me and wrinkled her forehead, causing little lines to form between her eyebrows. They made her look thoughtful, more grown up. I could tell she was deciding where to begin, so I let her contemplate as I waited.

"I met my parents." She said it almost casually. "My biological ones, I mean."

"Your parents?"

Whatever I had been expecting – it was unequivocally, unquestionably not this. I was sure that her parents were dead. She wasn't making any sense – no wonder she looked so befuddled. I generally always know what to say – but this? This I had no idea how to respond. So, I just stayed quiet.

She nodded, still looking down at her hands, making a sound of disgust.

"My parents. *Jonas* and *Myra*." She looked up at the last bit, directly into my eyes. Jonas and Myra, the names sounded familiar.

Benny. Yes. They were the ones Benny had mentioned, the evil ones who manipulated those people, scarred Benny, took his leg. Emilie's parents?

What could I say? I might have known most of the words in the dictionary, but none of them seemed of any use.

Emilie

I looked directly at him, wanting to watch his reaction. His eyes widened at the mention of their names, but it was in shock, not condemnation. He said nothing, and so I decided to continue. To tell him everything. And as I told him, I began to feel a little better, more able to straighten things out in my mind.

"And you believe them?" was all he said when I had finished.

"I – I don't know, Alphie. It's true that using my power was harder during training than it was when I first felt it. True that Etty hasn't been at all encouraging to you, in fact sometimes she's been downright discouraging. She didn't tell me about my parents, and she forbade me from talking about my experiences in the Rhisa. I honestly don't know what to think."

"Well, I do," Alphie retorted. It was the first time I had ever heard him speak so sharply, and it sliced right through me. Perhaps he noticed though, because he softened his tone as he continued. "I have lived with my grandmother since I was three years old. I know she may sometimes seem intimidating or discouraging, but she is not one jot. People are made of both good and bad, but her heart is solid."

"Your parents were killed, Alphie! She took you in

because she felt bad about the fight – maybe even guilty. I assume that's why she decided to have me for the summer too – to make amends for banishing my parents."

"Emilie!" His voice was raised well above its normal level of nicety, for good this time. "That's what *they* told you. Remember what Benny said. Jonas and Myra did horrible things. That's how my parents died. In fact, they still *are* doing horrible things. What sort of parents kidnap their daughter and her cousin and imprison them?"

I had to admit that despite Jonas and Myra wanting me to join them as their daughter, they hadn't exactly treated me like one so far. It was as if they didn't know how to. Did that make me feel pity for them, or suspicion? I couldn't decide.

"But they used to be different."

"Of course, they did – Grandmother loved Jonas and Myra, I'm sure she did," Alphie replied. "Why else did she keep at least one of their portraits, why else is it so hard for her to talk about them? They don't seem to find it hard to speak evil about *her*."

He had a point.

"Jonas and Myra…" I repeated, the words sounding lemony on my tongue, but there was something else there too.

"Look, it doesn't matter who they are, or what they believe, just who *you* are. And I am confident that you know Grandmother isn't like that. She's nothing like they told you she is."

I gave him a small, sad smile. I guess I knew it was true – I'd seen it hadn't I? Her occasional flashes of gentleness, her warmth as I hugged her when she declared it was time to start training. I guessed Alphie was right. Wasn't he?

"We need to get out of here, Emilie." His voice was now clothed in severity. "We need to warn Grandmother, to let her know that these people are still alive and still a threat."

"But these people are my parents, Alphie."

"How do you know that?" he insisted. "How do you know they aren't deceiving you in a vague attempt to get you to trust them?"

"I know they're my parents." As I said it I knew it was true. I couldn't explain how I knew but I did, I hoped he wouldn't ask. He didn't. Instead, he simply sighed.

"That may be. But we still need to get out, we still need to warn her."

"No!" I shouted and he seemed taken aback. "I can't just leave my parents."

"Emilie, if these people are who they say they are, then they must be evil. You heard what they did to Benny."

"And how do we know we can trust Benny? We don't know him either! But it's like you said, people have good and bad. And if my parents are bad, maybe I can bring out the good in them. Maybe I can change them." Perhaps it was the memory of the warmth of my father's hands which was making me so certain of myself, perhaps it was something else, but there was definitely something in my gut which was pushing confidence out of me and into my words.

Alphie sighed again. "I don't think that's how it works. People have to want to change in order to actually change. You can't just make them."

"Sure I can!" Now I was truly angry. He didn't understand. He was evidently far too taken up with Aunt Etty. But now that I had found out my parents were alive, that they were here, I couldn't just let them go. Not without trying. That was the one thing I was certain of.

"Fine, suit yourself."

Our conversation dissolved into silence. Unpleasant silence. Silence that was anything but calm. Silence that resounded with anger. I was fighting to shove back tears. I didn't want to argue with Alphie. I couldn't understand why he was unable to see how much this meant to me. He'd lost his parents too, hadn't he? What would he do if suddenly they were returned to him? For all his complicated words and sensitivities, he still couldn't understand how I was feeling. I went to lie on my bed in the corner, facing the wall so that I could let the tears fall and try to work out everything, tease out the knots that were forming in my mind and in my heart. Alphie sat on the other side. Back against the low table. Neither of us spoke.

CHAPTER FOURTEEN

Emilie

𝓣he next day, it was the same routine: we woke to breakfast already laid on the table. I wondered how they did it, whether someone unlocked the door and brought it in. But surely we'd have heard it? The only reasonable explanation was that magic was involved.

The silence that had wrapped itself around Alphie and me the night before still sat heavily in the air. We ate our breakfast in that same silence, Alphie's eyes intently focused on the toast, refusing to meet mine. I thought back to how we used to joke around together, comfort each other, work together. Everything had changed so quickly. I focussed on the floor and attempted to swallow. The food chundled down in lumps, and I could hear droplets of rain pounding against the skylight as I struggled through each bite.

Again, just as we were finishing (I had only managed half a slice) the cavern door opened. This time it was the black-jacketed guard who came to take me away. He was shorter and sturdier than the other one, but even he had a face just a bit too jolly to fit the villain stereotype. I suppose it was a good thing that the guards didn't look like they were straight out of a fairy tale – it helped me to remember that all this was really happening.

Alphie didn't stand this time to prevent me from leaving. I knew it was silly, but his resignation hurt. But, as if in regret, he offered me a small smile as I left.

"Remember who you are," he reminded me as I stepped through the door, each word weighted on his tongue.

I sighed. It wasn't that simple. I didn't know who I was – not really.

As I left the cavern, I steeled my determination to find the full truth – clearly this time, so I could prove Alphie wrong. Even Lizzie would have approved of such a logical approach. But thinking of Lizzie made my stomach scrunch. *Could I even call her my sister anymore?*

My parents - my biological parents - were waiting for me again in the long hall, this time settled into the chairs that seemed to be thrones. The one between them was empty.

"Come, sit." My mother's voice reverberated around the walls, young and strong. She laughed at the sound. I sauntered, or at least I tried to saunter, to the end of the room where they sat, and took the third chair which my father beckoned to.

It was for me.

"We thought we'd start your training now, if you're ready to join. No sense in waiting."

I jerked upright in shock. After all those weeks waiting for Etty to let me start training, here were my parents offering to start it immediately. I guessed they had faith in me. *So there Etty.* No, no – Alphie was right, Aunt Etty must have had a reason, and I was here for answers. Here to persuade my parents… but of what?

"Alphie said I shouldn't believe you."

The woman laughed again, this time with just the right amount of sweetness to make me feel foolish for doubting them.

"We thought he might say that. Etty has a way with words. The longer you stay with her the more you believe and trust her. Alphie has grown up with her. You mustn't blame him, Emilie. Even I was smitten with Etty, it took a lot of uncovering to discover that I had been misled."

"I *don't* blame Alphie." I was bitter in my defence.

"I see."

Silence again. But a softer silence, more friendly. As if they were waiting for me, but happy to wait.

"What sort of uncovering?" I finally said.

"All sorts," my mother replied. "The secrets of the Potensa that Etty has hidden for generations. We will

174

show them to you in training when you're ready. We will show you how to utilise your power without Etty's barriers and rules, how to become free. Invincible."

Alphie was right. The thought flashed through my mind. Invincibility generally led to evil. Generally. *But not always.* Besides, the curiosity to discover this new way was ever growing. It sounded easier than Etty's frustrating methods.

"Can Alphie learn too?"

"Would he want to?"

The question jarred me. I wasn't certain he would. It was true that he struggled with the way Etty taught, but I doubted he'd want my parents to teach him instead. I thought back to last night, the way he had refused to acknowledge them as my parents, the way he had immediately wanted to escape and tell Etty.

But my mother was already serving me an answer loud and clear: "He's got too much of Etty in him. But I think we may be able to find another use for him." My parents smiled at each other. "He's a leap day baby, isn't he?"

I nodded but hung back on her previous comment. *Was having too much Etty a bad thing?* The way my mother said it made it sound as if it was. But surely Alphie wasn't evil. That I was certain of.

"Alphie isn't evil."

"No, no of course not." My father glared at my mother. "Quite the opposite. He's got too much love in him; he can't see the evil in Etty because he loves her too much."

That I could understand. Alphie was full of love, always looking to see the best in people. He'd said that about me last night hadn't he: that it didn't matter who my parents were, it mattered who I wanted to be. In that instant I felt sorry for him. *Poor Alphie. Blinded by love.*

"In fact, I think it best you don't tell Alphie what we show you in training," continued my father with pronounced caution. "I don't think he's ready for it yet and we don't want him knowing too much. Maybe in time though he'll come to understand."

"Understand what?" I asked, not about to leave questions unspoken.

"That Etty is keeping your powers from you. She's keeping power from all the Potensa."

"What your mother means," my father interrupted, though his tone was laced in helpfulness, "is that we can help the Potensa." A gleam lit up his eye, his passion growing as he spoke. "Help all Potensa by getting rid of Etty's foolish ways. Help us come out of hiding. Help us take our rightful place in this world instead of cowering and covering our tracks from Ordinaries."

"Our rightful place?"

"Out of the shadows, into the light. So that the Ordinaries see us as …"

"Equals?" I suggested. My parents exchanged a glance, smiling at each other.

"Exactly …" said my father, his bottom lip curling ever so slightly.

I nodded and took a deep breath. Equality is always a good thing. That I'm certain of.

"Ok, I'm ready to learn."

They both gave me an encouraging smile. Pride churned in my stomach. My parents were pleased with me.

***

Alphie

Emilie's disappearance was further prolonged this time. I almost started to think that she wasn't coming back for me, that she had consigned me to oblivion, to death in this cavern. I didn't even know if they would feed me. After all, wasn't Emilie the one they wanted? In fact, I pondered at why they had even brought me here, if they just intended to keep me locked up. Surely, they knew I wouldn't let Emilie choose them without a tremendous fight.

It was a relief when one of the guards returned with lunch. Seemingly, they weren't going to let me starve. The guard smirked at me, turned, and left.

I ate the food as if each morsel was my last. I saw no reason for me to be kept alive in the cell, except maybe for Emilie's 'parents' to prove to her that they weren't so malevolent as to let her friend starve. *How ironic.* But I consoled myself with the knowledge that I would still be getting my three good meals a day. And indeed, this was a most delectable meal. Like that ploughman's lunch I had occasioned upon, on the day that Grandmother had taken me down to the village for my birthday. Etty had explained what a ploughman was, and I had mostly understood, something to do with farming, but the lunch had been very flavoursome, as indeed this one was.

I guessed Emilie was off eating with her newfound family. The thought pierced through my appetite. All of a sudden, I didn't want to finish my lunch.

I knew that I needed to escape. I was less certain now whether Emilie would come with me, but I chose to maintain faith in her. She had seemed to me to have chosen the light, hadn't she? But regardless of whether she would accompany me or not, I knew I had to flee. I knew I had to warn Grandmother.

A plan was necessary. I sat there, hunched over like a crested eagle, pushing hard into my thoughts.

***

Azariah

I felt blinded. It was an unsettling feeling for someone with the power of sight. There seemed to be a counter force that obscured Emilie from my sight.

We had been searching concentrated areas of Potensa power, and finally made it to some ruins of a castle in the Scottish Highlands. Etty knew that Jonas and Myra would choose a grand house that rivalled her own for their scheme, their attempt to topple her in whatever way they saw fit and break through her safety barriers so they could indulge in the power-hungry side of our Potensa gifts. She just hadn't guessed that they'd try to get Emilie back quite yet. Not when she was still so untrained.

I suppose I'd better tell you more of Emilie's backstory at this point. I do hope you understand why I avoided the subject before.

When Etty had heard through the chain of Potensa keeping a tab on Jonas and Myra that Emilie had been left at an orphanage, she had been overwhelmed with relief because it meant the child would grow up without their influence. Unfortunately for us, searching now for Emilie and Alphie's whereabouts, the spies had lost all trace of Emilie's parents soon after they left Emilie on that doorstep.

Myra and Jonas were too focussed on their ambition to want a daughter who might distract them. But now they were stronger, we were certain of it. Who knew what they had planned in the long-term? But the fact that they wanted control over all Potensa, the fact that they wanted Etty gone, the fact that they wanted even more power – that much was obvious.

Etty had known that Emilie would be better off without the weight of her parents' reputation, outside the world of the Potensa, and though it was hard, she waited until the girl was twelve years old before introducing her to it.

But now she was gone. And we had no idea where to. I couldn't see her anymore – the defensive barrier which blurred my vision was too strong. Jonas and Myra must have built some new defensive system around their stronghold. The travels which Etty and I had undertaken to find sources of concentrated Potensa power had led to nothing. So far we had been disappointed by three manor houses, two castles, and a couple of gothic estates. Most of them simply had large Potensa settlements nearby which caused their concentration of power. But at that moment, as we stood in the middle of nowhere, with no other Potensa even in sight, there was nothing but the biting weather to berate our failure.

Except, of course, the weather wasn't some sort of coincidental pathetic fallacy, some writing technique to set the mood.

It was Etty.

I hadn't seen Etty use her powers in years. Her sudden explosion of emotion unnerved me, for although she is more powerful than any Potensa I know, she rarely releases pent up energy through them. But at that moment the screeching wind was undeniably visible in her face as the weather twisted to her whim.

I closed my eyes and again tried to reach out to Emilie. I could see some fuzzy shapes moving about the vision, and radio crackling filled my ears. If only there were glasses for the mind, to allow me to pick out something of value from the scene. Emilie doesn't always read situations correctly, although she did seem to be somewhat improving. I worried for her all alone.

"We must move on." Etty's voice pulled me out of the vision. "We must keep looking."

I nodded solemnly, and we trudged our way back to the caravan.

It began to rain.

***

Alphie

I was beginning to feel again the pangs of hunger by the time the cavern door opened once more. Two figures entered. One came and removed the food, ignoring me in the corner. I suddenly wished I had eaten more. But the thought flew from me when I realised that the second figure was indeed Emilie. *Good – she hasn't forsaken me yet.*

She entered the room placidly, calmly, quite the contrary to her entry yesterday. It could have been my imagination, but she seemed older and harder. Was it the gathering dusk or was there a deeper blackness to her eyes, like the tiny flecks of green and blue were gone and replaced by streaks of black?

"What?" she said. I must have been staring at her for too long.

"Nothing," I brushed the thought away. "What happened? Where have you been?" I considered adding the phrase, "noble maiden" to the end of my statement as I once would have, but couldn't quite bring myself to do it.

"My parents offered me a room and suite upstairs near them, they said their daughter shouldn't be locked up."

"But you refused?"

"The invitation wasn't extended to you."

"I see." I had thought as much. Her refusal gave me hope though – the old, compassionate Emilie was still there. "Thank you," I added. She nodded.

"So," I tried broaching the subject again, "Pray tell, what new insights have your parents given you today?"

I said it with as much humour as I could muster but it still came out flat, bitter even.

***

Emilie

How was I supposed to tell him? Explain to him that my parents had told me my anger wasn't to be feared, that it was natural, that I could harness it and manipulate that anger rather than letting it manipulate me. I had eaten my first ever lunch with my biological parents and had spent the afternoon practising with light. I had controlled it better than I ever had before – causing little stars to grow in the air, glowing like tiny promising suns.

Both my parents (how that sounds!) also have power over light, and it turns out, over darkness as well. Get this – darkness is actually just as useful as light, if not more! We discussed the Rhisa at Etty's, and I finally had the courage to describe the pull to the darkness that had so long concerned me. They told me not to worry, that resisting the darkness was not worth the pain and energy it entailed, that instead I should let the darkness enter me so I could harness its power also. They had promised to show me their Rhisa and teach me how.

They had somehow replicated the light Rhisa from Etty's house and filled it with their power, although they refused to tell me how. I thought back to the great surge of energy I had experienced during training at Etty's, the memory tingling my fingers. If my parents had achieved such a creation, then who was I to refuse its help?

My parents had perfectly tied up the day by offering me a suite upstairs. I asked if Alphie could have one too, but they said that they couldn't trust him not to run away. I thought that if I could perhaps persuade him, we could both live here together.

I had seen the glint of their hopeful eyes when I confirmed that Alphie was born on a leap day. They offered me their enthusiasm to set up a Rhisa for him, to rear his power in.

But now, with Alphie's frown facing me, I suddenly didn't know what to say. My parents had warned me not to tell Alphie what we did in training or about the Rhisa. I had agreed that to do so would be foolish. Not because

I wanted to be a dutiful daughter but because I somehow didn't think Alphie would approve.

"They said you could have a bedroom too," I defended them, knowing it wasn't really an answer to his question, merely the only response I could muster. "If you promised not to run away, that is."

He snorted. "I see – bribery."

"No, it's not bribery. They just want what's best for you but don't think you're ready for it yet."

He snorted again, this time louder. His harshness scraped against me. "What – the same way they want what is best for you, but Grandmother is coming between that?"

"Alphie!" I shouted. That got his attention. "I used my powers again today. I was stronger, more capable with their teaching. They're willing to train you too, they've got a Rhisa for my power and they want to set one up for you. Please say you'll co-operate. We can be happy here, the two of us. We can be a real family, they can be your parents too, I know they would, please just say yes."

He looked like I had just slapped him. Shock, confusion, and could I sense a frothing anger? Surely not, Alphie was never angry.

"They have Rhisa of their own?"

"Well, yes. I haven't actually seen them yet, but they told me they'd show me tomorrow. But that's not what's important – please just say you'll stay."

"Emilie, do you not see what that means?"

Obviously, I didn't. "If they have Rhisa too that means that they have a source for the powers too. And I dread to think of how they created them – no Potensa would volunteer to give their power to these Rhisa as they would for those of the Head, they must have taken those powers by force. This could jeopardise our world as we know it, everything my grandmother has striven towards. There's a reason that the Head alone has the Rhisa."

"So what!" I almost screamed. Being loud was filling in the cracks in my certainty. "Can't you see that's the problem? Etty has total control over our powers and she sets limits to keep us weak, to keep us in line, can't you see that?"

"No, I can't." His voice was so cool, so controlled, so unlike him. "She has boundaries to keep us safe. You saw what happened to Benny. When boundaries are crossed, people get hurt. Appearances are deceitful, Emilie. This isn't one of your storybooks where everything is black and white."

That hurt. How dare he make me feel like a child.

"The knights don't wear shining armour and the villains don't breathe fire. You're scaring me, Emilie. You can't see what's happening to you, how they're manipulating you. But I can, and it's tearing me apart."

I didn't know what to say to that. I wanted to believe my parents, wanted to be a part of this with them.

"And what about your real parents?" he continued.

"These are my real parents."

"No, they're not, Emilie. Where were they when you took your first step or when you said your first word or when you had your first princess party? Your *real* parents sent you to Grandmother's, doesn't that mean you can trust *them*, even if you can't trust *her*?"

I felt tears seeping into my vision; what he had said was true. Hadn't I wondered why my biological parents hadn't escaped from Aunt Etty *with* me, rather than leaving me on the doorstep of an orphanage, and why they were only now connecting with me after twelve years? I could feel an uncomfortable knot building in my throat and stomach.

"That's the point though, isn't it?" I said, all anger leaving me. "I don't know who to trust." Defeat dropped my head and that's when the tears properly came. Then Alphie was at my side and holding me as if I were a porcelain doll about to break. Maybe I was about to break.

I rocked back and forth in the warmth of his arms, letting the tears fall without hesitation. "You can trust me," he whispered, "I have the beginnings of a plan."

"I can't leave them," I whispered back through the tears.

"You have to."

"I can't."

He didn't argue anymore but just let me cry. Eventually my tears were spent.

CHAPTER FIFTEEN

Emilie

By morning, certainty grounded my stomach; I knew what I had to do. Before I could decide who to believe, I needed the facts, and I needed to see the Rhisa. I don't know why, but I felt that the Rhisa would show me answers. Alphie wouldn't understand. I knew he wouldn't, but I didn't expect such resistance.

"No way!" he exclaimed, flinging his toast back onto his plate, almost knocking over his full cup of water. "We shouldn't remain on the premises a day more, Emilie. We've been here two days and look how it's already affected you, look how it's already infected your demeanour." He gestured to my face; it must have looked awful after my sleepless night.

"But surely it's best to know all of the facts first."

"Facts? It all boils down to who you trust, who you

give credence to. And I don't trust your parents, sorry."

"Well, I don't trust your grandmother – *sorry*," I replied, bitterly mimicking his wording.

"So that's your choice?"

No – it wasn't quite – I was still confused, still wishing I could just curl up in a ball and forget everything. But I didn't know how to put that into words, so I just said, "Yes, that's my choice."

"Fine, well I wish-"

The door to the cavern clanged open, interrupting whatever he was about to say. The guard arrived, smirking as ever. I rose without looking at Alphie. I didn't want to see his face, didn't want to see the disappointment or accusation or whatever it was he was showing.

But as the door was locked behind me, I heard Alphie call out, "Farewell dearest Emilie, I hope you trust me."

I didn't respond.

***

Alphie

I don't think either of us had slept properly that night. We just lay there, side by side, lost to our thoughts. But Emilie's murmuring was eventually snuffed out and, in the silence, I had been able to clasp together the vague form of a plan in my mind. I was pretty sure I could make it out of the cavern, but who knew how I would fare afterwards? Emilie had told me about the corridor and the hall at the far right of it, so I guessed that left was the most appropriate escape route. It was a risk, but I was beginning to familiarise myself with the notion of uncertainty.

Regret at planning to leave Emilie behind made me falter, but over the course of our brief time together I had become well acquainted with her stubbornness. It was a virtue, most definitely, but also a flaw. When she had said, last night, that she wasn't leaving her parents, there was a directness to her gaze that told me nothing I could say would change her mind.

Emilie was beyond my help, even the most eloquent persuasion of mine wouldn't be able to reach her now. The best thing I could do for her was to get out of here myself and to gather a rescue team. There was a new glint in her eye when she spoke of her parents which unnerved me – made me more eager to leave, even without her. Besides, who knew what Jonas and Myra could do if they had the power of the Rhisa?

I was also conscious that it wouldn't be long before Emilie told them of my power. It wouldn't be long before they tried to use me. Maybe that's what all the disappearances of Potensa had been caused by. Most people thought the disappearances were rumours and tall tales, but I had been able to tell from Etty's response as Head that they were not. Now it all made sense. Most probably they had been kidnapped, brought here, and forced to give over their powers to a Rhisa. It all made sense. I felt a deep dismay and dread wash over me, filling me with the urge to vomit. I looked around the cavern with new eyes. How many had been kept here, imprisoned, tormented, petrified and alone? I doubted they had been given lavish furnishings as we had, but it wasn't hard to guess how terrifying the cavern would be without the rug and the beds and the table to soften it. I was suddenly grateful that I was not solitary and alone but inadvertently under Emilie's protection. But I knew that wouldn't last long. Greed has a certain impatience to it, and leap day Potensa are highly unusual. And, supposedly, powerful. I wasn't just brought here because I happened to be with Emilie.

I was brought here for a purpose.

I had been fearful all along, but now panic strained at my chest. I needed to get away. And as soon as possible. Vamoose – that was the word. I needed to vamoose.

I had likely been too strident with Emilie this morning, too merciless. I knew that if my plan failed and I was caught escaping, I would be lucky if the worst fate that befell me was being thrown back in this cavern. I thought of what had happened to Benny, the stump where there should have been a leg. Surely Emilie wouldn't let them do that to me? But then again – she might never know if they did. She'd be told that I had absconded and abandoned her. What would she think of me?

Adventuring had never really been my thing. I had of course scampered into mischief but not for any daring escapades, more for silly practical jokes. I didn't like to think that I was merely being a frightened child, but I have to admit that fear was the overriding emotion I was chained in. But perhaps it was actually rooted in sadness, for the pit of my stomach weighed me downwards all the while. I wished my parting from Emilie had been kinder, sweeter, a hug maybe, not bitter words and turned backs.

But I had a plan to focus on. A plan that would hopefully work. I turned to my undrunk cup of water on the breakfast table and hid it behind the bed. Hopefully they wouldn't miss the cup when they came to take away the remains of the breakfast.

***

Emilie

My parents were waiting for me in the hall again, smiles wide. I drifted over to them, still stewing on Alphie's words. But their smiles drew the frown from my face, and I went to embrace them. They were colder than Alphie's arms had been last night, stiffer. But they were still my parents.

"Are you ready?" my father asked.

I nodded, bottom lip clamped between my teeth. He smiled encouragingly and together the three of us walked back towards the door I had just entered. We walked back down the corridor – the guards were nowhere to be seen. The corridor was long and straight, ending in another door. We walked past the door to the cavern; I thought with a pang of Alphie sitting there alone. But with my father's hand placed on my shoulder, the pang soon spiralled to anger as I remembered my parents' kind offer to train him, and his refusal. He'd chosen his way and I'd chosen mine.

We continued down the corridor; I concentrated on the sounds of three pairs of footsteps, all related by blood. How marvellous the thought of our shared genes sounded in my head. There were no other doors that I could see apart from the one at the end. My curiosity as to what lay behind it tumbled about in my stomach, growing as it twisted and turned. But before we could reach it, my parents gently nudged me to the right, and I saw a staircase clambering straight up, rather like Etty's staircase. I had been too fixated on the door to notice it before.

"What's behind that door?" I asked, pointing to the one at the end, curiosity getting the best of me.

"Oh, nothing exciting, that's where Harry and Bill stay."

I assumed Harry and Bill were the guards. At least I now knew what to call them. I felt a small pang of guilt for thinking about them so rudely in my head before.

"The really exciting bit is up here!"

I turned and followed my mother up the staircase, my father drawing close behind me. I made a mental note to beg them for a tour of the whole place later on.

We reached the top of the stairs and I felt like I had been transported back to the top floor at Etty's that midnight with Alphie. Everything was exactly the same, right down to the circular pattern on the carpet. I could hear the hum of the Rhisa, feel the rush in my hands.

We moved as one to stand in front of the fourth door from the end, the exchange of words unnecessary. I noted that the door to the Rhisa opposite was flung wide open, painted grey inside and empty. I guessed that meant it was unfinished. A couple of doors matched the description, but the other doors, all closed tight, must have been ready and working. My parents stood either side of me as I leant towards the humming door.

"You're coming in with me?"

My mother nodded. "Of course."

I smiled, opened the door and stepped inside.

***

Azariah

I couldn't see her anymore. Not at all. None of Etty's guesses about her whereabouts came to any fruition.

I thought I'd have to give up on her; I didn't know what else to do. Without her, I was lost.

I'm sorry; don't expect to hear much more from me for a while. I saw nothing for days.

***

Alphie

As I accurately predicted, the guard entered and took away the breakfast not long after Emilie had departed. He didn't say anything about the cup, which I hoped meant that he hadn't perceived its absence. I knew time was against me and so I unveiled the cup from behind the bed and set it down directly below the lock to the door, cursing as I let some water spill.

The idea of the cup's usage had come to me during the tiny cracks of some broken dreams, when I remembered how I had once left the lid on a pot of boiling water during an escapade with the twins by their caravan and forgotten about it until all of a sudden it had popped off and scared the living daylights out of us all. I knew that working with the cup of water would be different, would be more challenging by far, but it was my only chance.

I stared intently at the cup, remembering doing the same on the front lawn outside Grandmother's manor. I brought to mind the joy of my success, and of that mirrored in Emilie as she watched me, the smile that lit up the tiny flecks in her eyes. I was doing this for her. I blocked out everything around me and pressed hard with my mind, seeing and feeling the spiral of water rise from the cup as it had before. But this time, rising was not enough. Slowly, I directed the flow towards the lock. I could tell I didn't have enough power, that I was running out of energy, my attempts lacklustre. Desperate now, I directed the water back over the cup and let it fall. Failure.

I sat back in despair, simply wanting to wallow in my foundering. But that was what *they* wanted me to do. Jonas and Myra. They thought I wouldn't be strong enough, potent enough, skilled enough to escape. They were banking on my weakness. I would prove them wrong. I counted to sixty. That was time enough. Emilie wouldn't want me to give up, Grandmother wouldn't, the twins wouldn't, my parents wouldn't – if only they were alive to see me now. They had loved me; they had died for me, for our way of life. Grandmother needed me; Emilie couldn't see it, but she too needed me. I couldn't fall short now.

I attempted once again, this time bringing to mind everything I loved about the natural world: the whisper of the breeze between the leaves, the dart of a brook through a clearing, the scent of overturned dirt, the warmth of a fire at night. That reminded me of Emilie, her silliness at insisting on having hot chocolate in front of the fire, despite the warmth of the day. I was smiling now, I could feel it, and with that smile dancing I mustered all the strength, courage and fortitude I had and pushed it into the water.

I commanded it to move, and it acquiesced. I pumped as much of the water as possible into the keyhole, feeling the resistance of the metal against me. What I really needed was some heat to enkindle the water to expand, but heat was too close to fire and I couldn't control that yet.

Yet. The word stuck in my mind. Courage ballooned my chest. Now seemed like the best time to try. I tried to bring fire to my mind, imagined it burning, heating the water from below.

But to no avail. To dwell on my failing would be counterproductive, and so I sped on to a different approach.

I put my mind to focusing specifically on the water. I had filled the keyhole with all the water I could from the cup, but still it was not enough. I closed my eyes, focusing on all the water around me and suddenly I could sense it: the droplets in the air around. I directed those too towards the keyhole, pushing with all my might. I had begun to sweat, and I directed the beads of sweat there too.

I knew it was dangerous, I had never gone this far, never taken water from my own body. I felt again the resistance of the metal of the mechanism, felt as if I was the water, trapped in a tiny hole, pushing and shoving to get out against the pressure of metal. The sensation of pushing was reflected by the fear sweeping up inside of me.

Then I heard Emilie's cheer in my mind, her words from so long ago as we practised together: "Almost there Alphie, come on, you can do it, one final push." And so, push I did. The lock split in half along a joint and fell apart with a spurt of water. And I was laughing and crying and soaked by its iciness. I lay down, breaths heavy. I could feel the pressure of a headache building in my head and I didn't want it to explode. So, with the little strength I had left, I directed some of the water back into the cup. It wasn't clean, but it was cold and I drank gratefully.

I gave myself five minutes of repose before I stood again. I reckoned it was safe, prudent even, to do so – the past couple of days the guards hadn't come back until lunch.

I inclined my ear to the door, listening intently but no sound reached me. Whether that was because the coast was clear or because the door was too thick for sound to travel through – I couldn't tell.

I opened the door gently, wincing as the metal clanged, sending rumblings back through the cavern. There was nobody outside. The corridor was empty. The carpet was pleasant, the wood dark.

I could see one door at either end of the corridor, the one to the right closer to me. If anyone came out of that I was utterly and unavoidably trapped. So, I turned left instead, and made my way as rapidly as my tired bones would allow to the corridor's culmination. Towards its end, the forgiving carpet muffling my footsteps, I passed a small flight of stairs. They looked strangely familiar, and I considered chancing a look. But I shoved down my curiosity – the way out was definitely not upstairs. If Emilie was here, I knew she would have ascended and peered at what lay above, but rampant curiosity had no place in my plan. I reached the end of the corridor and leant into the door. This door was wooden not metal, and through it I could hear vague murmuring.

"One of the cups is missing, Bill."

So, they had noticed.

"Don't think it matters too much."

I heaved a relief-sunken sigh.

"No, probably not, but it's better to be safe than sorry."

No, no, no.

"The boy was probably just thirsty, give it a break."

"I don't doubt it, but I better check. The bosses said to keep an extra special eye on him."

"Suit yourself, I'll keep washing."

He was coming, I could hear footsteps approaching the door. I couldn't run back, the door at the other end of the corridor led straight to the hall, and I doubted I could make the hundred or so metres in time. I was stuck. I would be caught and apprehended.

The staircase. The thought flashed through my mind in an instant and I ran, ducking into the alcove where the stairs were partially blocked from view and running up them three at a time. I peered down as the man tramped past, he didn't seem to see me and continued onwards to the cavern. I felt a surge of relief but that was quickly exchanged for panic – it would take him all of half a minute to realise that I was gone. I saw him open the door and as soon as he had disappeared, I mustered all of my strength. The air in the corridor began to swirl and as I focused it intently I heard the door slam. Another thrust of power and I hoped it would momentarily jam.

I didn't wait to see. I jumped down the stairs using the bottom banister as a propellant and hurtled back to the door where I'd perceived the voices. There was undoubtedly still someone behind the door – I had heard his voice – but I hoped I had the advantage of surprise.

This was going wrong. So wrong.

I gritted my teeth and wrenched open the door.

CHAPTER SIXTEEN

Emilie

*T*his Rhisa felt different, in a way I couldn't quite explain. It felt somehow forceful, stronger, and rather than feeling like home, it felt like a castle. Strong, powerful, immovable.

My mother spoke from beside me. Her voice jolted me. It was the same voice that had whispered to me in the Rhisa at Etty's, the voice that had called to me and enticed me. I knew, when my father next spoke, that I had heard his voice too.

"See if you can control it. Don't just feel it but use it, manipulate it, bind the light to your will."

Etty's command to be cautious, to feel the power and do nothing else flashed through my mind, fighting with that of my father's. I guessed that was another one of her silly barriers.

I drew the light to me, relishing in its resistance to my command. This time, rather than gently coiling around me, I pulled it to me. I had the control, not it. I was no longer helpless to the power and whims of the Rhisa.

"Very good," my father's voice slithered into my ear. "Keep going, don't let it resist you, show it who the powerful one is."

I strained harder, drawing the power in through my hands, my face, every inch of me, pulling and reaching, but still it resisted.

"Just come to me," I screamed, anger burning through my bones, and with the anger came the hot white light. I thought of Alphie's comment this morning, Alphie, who I thought was my friend, who I thought cared for me, but refused to trust my parents. A roar of rage pulsed through me and I yanked on the light, dragging it towards me, sucking it from the Rhisa.

There was a flash, like that of a light bulb bursting, and then darkness.

I heard my father chuckle beside me. It was not an evil sound, but for some reason it echoed shakily through my ears. The darkness pressed down on me and I let it. I didn't know what I had done, or whether it could be reversed, but I didn't care. I had the power; I had the control. I felt empty. But invincible. My mother reached for my hand, curling her fingers around mine.

***

Alphie

As I jerked open the door, I heard a roar from the cavern – muffled but unambiguous. I only hoped that the other guard hadn't registered it. I had all of twenty seconds to take in my surroundings – a kind of dining or living room, not wholly uncouth, nor unpleasant. A door to my left was hanging wide open and I could hear whistling and the sound of crockery being clanged together – presumably the second guard. Across, on the other side of the room, was another door. This assumed the appearance of what might be an exterior door, leading to the outside. It wasn't over yet.

"Told you it was nothing, Bill," came a voice from the door on the left.

It was the man washing up. He must have heard me infiltrate their quarters. I scampered across the room, dodging a dark grey ottoman, and made it to the door. By now though, my hands were shaking so abominably that it would not open. For one bloodcurdling moment I thought that it might be locked, but I finally summoned the stillness to grab its handle, and it swung open with ease. A shout from behind. I paused. Just long enough to summon a blast of air which I hoped would overturn some furniture.

I was out. I had made it outside. But it now became

apparent that despite being outside I was still trapped. My stomach felt like lead. I was in a dirt-floored courtyard, and ahead of me loomed a large iron gate that looked to be at least twice my height.

I darted across the empty space, mind furiously whirling. I had banked on more time to plan my route spontaneously as I went along. I hadn't anticipated my absence being noticed so soon.

Think, think, think.

It was like a riddle: ponder hard enough and an answer would materialise. And as I ran, I felt the ground soft and pliable beneath my feet – it must have been raining recently.

And then the idea came to me.

I dashed forwards, once again mustering as much strength and vitality as I could. Apart from fire, controlling the earth was the power that I struggled most with during training. Yet in that instant I knew I could do it. I had to. I had come so far, so close to freedom – I couldn't let myself be caught and once again incarcerated. I refused to let them beat me. I remembered Grandmother's warning, from training, that I wouldn't always have earth right under me, but now I did. And the sodden soil was the perfect instrument, the moisture making it more transferable. I knew I didn't have long, a few seconds maybe, before the guards would be upon me.

There was nothing for it. I pushed all the energy I could assemble into the ground under the gate, willing it to move, and to my utter astonishment it did. The soil was pushed back and exploded around the edges on the other side of the gate, leaving a perfect tunnel. I widened it a little and then dived, wriggling and squirming. I felt like a worm, trapped under a shoe, desperately and hopelessly trying to escape. But the desperation paid off. I jerked free of the shoe, under and out of the gate.

Raising myself up, I swivelled around; both men had now appeared at the door and were running towards the gate. One shouted something inaudible to the other, who turned and headed in the opposite direction. I didn't have time to wonder, all thoughts consumed by the next impediment that would come my way. I reckoned the man wouldn't be small enough to make it through the hole, so I left it there. He'd be forced to open the gates to apprehend me, to catch me – and I begged it would be a lengthy process. I didn't wait to find out.

I turned. I was in a field that sloped down into a copse of trees a couple of hundred metres away. That seemed my best hope of cover and I sprinted towards it, slowing as I entered. Running didn't usually tire me out, so it must have been the combined usage of my power which was exhausting me. I wanted to throw up but forced myself to keep going on through the trees, hobbling as fast as I could.

I heard barks behind me – dogs. That must have been why the other man disappeared. I felt around for the moisture in the ground, knowing that if I had the strength, I could summon the water to the surface and create a kind of shallow lake to cover my tracks and scent. But a coughing fit overwhelmed me as I wrenched against my depleted, emptied energy, and I knew in that instant I had neither the strength, nor the skill, nor the time.

Was this how it was going to end? After all of the struggle, after I had made it out past the gates, was I to be hunted down by dogs? And then I heard it – the low hum of rushing water. I once again engaged my power, reaching out with my mind, and I sensed a stream that couldn't be very far, probably just on the other side of the trees. I let out a moan which flowed from my gut to my head, both of relief and pain. Relief that there was a way out, pain that I must once again force my exhausted limbs to run.

I raced through the trees, missing the majority of the low-lying branches. I was hastened onwards by the wretched sound of snarling dogs behind me. *Keep going, keep going.* I made it to the river and waded downstream. The force of the water was pushing me forwards. I succumbed and let it carry me.

Peering over my shoulder, I could see three dogs standing tall on the bank, the fourth dog adrift in the river. The water seemed to be pounding against its form. Its focus was no longer on me, but on struggling back to shore. I almost felt sorry for its straggling limbs.

I stumbled out of the darkness of the Rhisa and into the lull of the corridor. Even here, the light seemed to have left. Had I done that? My mother lifted her hand, pushing the light back into the lamps along the top of the wall. I could see my parents looking at each other in satisfaction. Then my father turned to me. The pride his face was lit with suddenly reflected in my own. I had made my parents proud. All of a sudden, I didn't care what I had done, whether drawing the light to me was bad. Not only did I feel more powerful than ever before, my fingers still pulsing with electrified energy from the Rhisa, but I was also standing between my parents. Parents who were proud of me, who allowed me to be who I was and didn't keep secrets from me.

"Would you like to try out some more Rhisa?"

"What, go into the Rhisa of other Potensa?" I hadn't thought that was possible! I guessed it was another of Etty's rules to hold us back. The thought itself pulled my eye to the other doors, and an urge to see what Potensa of different months did inside their Rhisa flooded through me.

"Yes. We believe that harnessing more than one power isn't just something that leap day Potensa can do. We think we might even be able to harness all of them. We thought that you, as our special daughter, might be the first to try it."

I had no words.

"Of course, only if you want to," my father quickly added.

I nodded vigorously. I guess curiosity had always been my biggest flaw. But maybe I should embrace that trait, just like I had with the darkness?

"Which one do you want to try first?"

I suddenly realised that I didn't even know all the powers that existed. But I still knew which I'd like to have the most.

"Alphie's." I had always been nagged by an interest in what he saw in his Rhisa. Perhaps even a small, sheltered part of me also wanted to see if his powers were as hard to use as he made out.

"Unfortunately, we don't have Alphie's Rhisa yet. We're hoping he might help us out with that in due course. Perhaps you could talk to him again later?"

I nodded. Then another thought bobbed up in my brain.

"What's Etty's power?"

My dad laughed outright. "That's my girl. It's the weather. Would you like to try it?"

"Have you tried it?"

He seemed to craft his answer carefully. "We've tried many of the Rhisa, but so far, we've not been successful. We're hoping that a younger mind, one that is still growing and developing, will be able to find the triumph we couldn't."

It sounded fair enough (and of course I liked the idea of a triumph!).

My parents steered me to one of the closed doors. I was the one to open it, it seemed my parents didn't lock their Rhisa as Etty had, and together we stepped in. It was strange, very strange, stranger even than my Rhisa and any sense of familiarity was gone. We were in an open field, blue sky met by yellow-tinged grass, and I could feel a gentle breeze swirling around me, disturbing the stalks at my heels. My parents didn't seem as amazed as I was; they must have been in here before.

"What do I do?"

"I suggest focusing on one aspect of the weather and trying to change that." My mother's voice was bathed in milky encouragement.

It sounded so simple.

I spotted a cloud outlined against the blue and focused on that, pouring my energy into making it grey, to fill it with rain, which could fall and water the earth. *How hard could it be?* Nothing happened for a minute or two, but then the cloud did begin to expand and darken. Or maybe that was just my imagination. I pushed harder, willing it on with all my might. It had to work, my parents were counting on me, they believed I could do it. I could feel the energy leaving me, a gallon of energy for each new drop I tried to add to the foamy-white bundle. Something was wet, but it was me, not the cloud. Sweat, so much sweat. I suddenly felt lightheaded, but still I kept pushing, desperately hoping to please my parents. A buzzing in my ear. I could feel the field slipping away. Was that rain or was that my vision blurring?

Once again, for the second time that week I saw black.

***

Emilie

I could hear dogs barking in the distance, echoing around my head as well as through the halls. The sound brought me back to reality. I was lying on the floor in the corridor. I hadn't been able to do it. I had failed. I looked up to see the underside of my parents' chins pushed forwards, hushed tones passing between them. I tried to talk.

"I'm sorry," I managed to whisper, and sat up.

"Never mind dear, that was only your first time, I'm sure you'll get better." It was supposed to be encouraging.

I wasn't so sure. But then one of the guards was there, scuttling up the stairs. He had a run that reminded me of those little crabs on the beach, like he didn't much like being out in the open and couldn't wait to find his next hole to scamper into. He approached my father and whispered to him; my mother leaned in to hear too.

I watched my mother's face turn grim; lines extended

across her forehead and pulled down the corners of her mouth. The news obviously couldn't be good. She bent over so that her face was no longer visible. When she turned again, the cold look was back.

"Emilie," my father said, with all the benevolence that he could muster. It still came out rather flat. "I'm afraid Alphie has abandoned us. He ran away this morning."

Abandoned. The word pulsed through me. I was very familiar with the feeling.

Alphie was supposed to be the sensitive one, the caring one, the one who was cheery, full of quirks. And now he had abandoned me. He had meant this morning's goodbye very literally. And I had said nothing. I found myself lying again on the floor, the emptiness from the corridor now magnifying through every part of me.

I knew I couldn't deal with the emptiness. It throbbed in an unbearable way. So, I let the anger seep through and replace it. It smarted, but in a way that felt right, in a way that pounded through me and bolstered me. I had trusted Alphie – look where it had left me. I had trusted Etty, now I knew that was stupid too. I had trusted my adopted parents, but they had sent me away to Etty. I had trusted Lizzie, but all her sensible beliefs had been proven untrue. I trusted my biological parents, but what did I really know about them?

No. *The only person I can trust is myself.*

I felt that truth seep through me like ice and as Myra

leant to put her arms around me, I wrenched myself free from her grasp. Nobody else. Just me.

And then that ice turned to fire and I was burning with anger, about to incinerate and destroy everything close to me – and I almost wished I would. The force of my anger pounded in my ears and as I roared, the light bulbs shattered, and we were once again plunged into darkness.

CHAPTER SEVENTEEN

Alphie

After approximately five minutes in the river, I decided that I was far enough away from the dogs. Besides, the previously gentle rocking of the waves had morphed into an icy bite. Working my way to the bank, I found a foothold in a twisted root and heaved myself out. The bank was soft, and I let it envelope me as I recovered my breath. Rising, I noticed with dismay that I had left a body sized imprint in the damp ground of the bank. Oh well, I would just have to trust that I had the advantage of time and speed.

Straining my ears, I could just about make out a distant purr, one that sounded like far-off cars. Cars meant a road, and a road meant a ride. I had never hitchhiked before, but I knew the routine.

I reached the road, without misadventure. It was

around midmorning, and there were a sizable number of cars going in both directions. I had no idea which way was home, but I only really had two options. I tried flagging down a couple of cars, but they all drove past, apathetic, disregarding me. I was beginning to feel nervous – if the men had followed me, then it would be easy to see where I had left the river and obvious that I would head to the road. That gave me three minutes, or maybe five at most. A van was nearing, and I must have looked desperate as I waved because it pulled over.

"Where you off to, son?" The driver seemed friendly enough.

"I'm heading back home, to the house on the hill near Appledown." I was beginning to feel a little shaky; my voice sounded weedy, insubstantial.

It was with growing astonishment that the driver informed me that I was all but nine miles away and that he could happily drop me in the village next to Appledown. I couldn't believe my luck that we were so close to home. After all, Jonas and Myra could have taken us anywhere. And I knew the village he was talking about; it would be easy to fathom my way back from there.

I readily agreed.

"No worries, you look like you need a ride. Hop in." Positively exuding relief, I clambered aboard. Grandmother would know what to do when I arrived back, she always did.

"Where exactly are we now?" I inquired

nonchalantly, although my pulse maintained a panicked rhythm in my head.

"Pretty much in the middle of nowhere. Closest village, Dalehead, is three miles back, where I've just come from. Beats me how you ended up here. What were you doing – some youthful exploring?" His grin was echoed in his words.

"Something like that."

"Suit yourself." He shrugged; eyes focussed on the road.

Dalehead. I needed to remember that. I would tell Grandmother where Emilie was being kept, and she would know how to rescue her. I had faith in my grandmother. And I had faith in Emilie to make the right decisions. At least, I hoped she would.

The drive should have only taken ten minutes but, thanks to some cattle blocking the road, it ended up taking thrice that and I found myself nodding off a little. After a while, we stopped.

"I'm afraid this is as far as I can bring you. If you go into the post office, they could probably show you the path to Appledown, otherwise you could see if you could catch another lift."

I hopped down, thanking the driver, and headed into the village. Its name was spelt in flowers on the green and I easily spotted the post office.

The sun was now high in the sky, and I made it out to be around noon. I had the foresight to ask for directions back to Dalehead just in case, and, with both sets of directions jotted down on my hand from a kindly lent pen, I set out into the fields along a public bridleway. With the late August sun reigning down, it would have been a pleasant walk, in other circumstances, but now the few miles to Grandmother's manor seemed endless, my pace never fast enough. I began to recognise the fields after approximately twenty minutes of walking and could tell that I was once again in home territory. I took an unscripted left at the next break in the path, knowing that it would take me directly home rather than through the village. When I neared the bottom of the drive, I began to run, the promise of an end to my journey spurring me on.

I bounded up to the front door and beat on it with all my might. I had made it.

No answer. I beat again.

"Grandmother, Grandmother, it's me – Alphie." Again, no answer. "Can you hear me? Etty, Grandmother, it's me – Alphie."

Silence.

Confusion flooded through me. Where was she? I knew from experience that if she were inside, she would have heard me. Loud knocks on the huge doors reverberated through the whole house, even up to the attic. She must be in the garden.

I rushed round the back, screaming her name and emitting a thousand tiny prayers in all directions that she was there. It felt like a nightmare. My steps lagging, my cries unanswered, I ran along and along the path, towards the archway and the Darwala. She must just be in there. I dashed through the Darwala, noting nothing but how long it was. I emerged at the other end, on top of the hill and almost bumped into two figures.

"Alphie," they cried, enveloping me in hugs.

It was the twins; they must have been waiting for something.

"Where's Emilie? Or Etty?" Zander cried, looking behind me as if waiting for them to emerge.

"What?" I panted. "I came to ask you the same thing."

"You mean they're not with you?" Lori butted in immediately, fear distorting her face.

"No, I came here to find Grandmother."

"But how did you get here? Etty said you had been taken."

"I escaped."

Admiration flashed across their faces.

"And Emilie?"

"She … she didn't want to come." The words hurt as they escaped my mouth, leaving little open wounds all up my throat.

"Oh dear," was all Lori could say. "Oh dear, this is very bad."

"I know!" I said, trying to keep the panic out of my voice. "Where's my grandmother?"

"We don't know, she's not here, she went off to find the two of you. You'd better come home with us."

Not here. The words sunk in and settled like lead. I

had no idea what to do, I needed Grandmother to tell me. She obviously didn't know where to look if she hadn't found us. I felt so alone.

***

Alphie

The twins led me through the maze of caravans towards theirs. None of us spoke, I guess we were all trying to figure out what to do next, desperately wanting someone to tell us, for an adult to step in and absolve us, free us of all responsibility. The twins always said that they only used their caravan when they were lazy or there was an emergency. I guessed this was an emergency.

The garish colours of the afternoon sun boiled against me. We walked inside the caravan. The twins did the clicks. I thought back to the last time we'd done this, to Emilie's shock, excitement, confusion, joy. The laughter on her face. And then I thought back to her face this morning: bitter, tired, pale. I could feel my eyes stinging but this was not the time to cry. She needed me to be strong. We exited the caravan, into the garden of the Sanders' household, and we were no sooner through the door than Mrs Sanders pounced on us.

"Alphie, thank goodness you're alive! I've been so worried, where's Emilie?"

Then my tears really came.

She drew me into her arms and gave me a mother-swathed minute, peering over my head to where the twins were explaining in hushed, fearful tones what I had told them.

"We'd best come inside and discuss everything." Mrs Sanders' voice was gentle. "Are you hungry?"

I nodded, following her to the kitchen and wiping my face on the back of my sleeve. The clock in their kitchen read three o'clock. I hadn't eaten since breakfast. As if in response to that realisation, my stomach growled. Mrs Sanders sat me down and went about preparing the food, allowing me to recompose myself and pull myself together. Lori and Zander followed, taking chairs on the other side of the table, concern written across their faces. Ally was on the floor and crawled over to me. I scooped her up and held her tight, feeling her warmth and softness against me.

She wriggled out of my arms as Mrs Sanders brought over a cup of tea and some sandwiches. *Tea.* What a mother's thing to add. I didn't think even tea could solve this problem though.

"So, you haven't seen Etty?" Mrs Sanders started.

I shook my head. "Where'd she go?" I said, my voice sounding more desperate than I had intended.

"She sent a message three evenings ago that you and Emilie had been captured and that she and Azariah were going to find you." I didn't know who Azariah was, but I didn't have the effort to ask. "She said she didn't know where you'd been taken but that she had a couple of ideas. Obviously not the right ones if you haven't seen her."

Mrs Sanders paused, and levelled her tone. "What happened, Alphie?"

I told them everything, right up to reaching the house and finding it empty. Fabian entered partway through and just stood in the doorway, listening.

"We have to go back for her, we have to get her out," I said then slumped back in my chair, the very picture of defeat.

"I don't think it's going to be that easy, Alphie, I'm sorry," Mrs Sanders responded. "You said yourself she didn't want to leave, and you going back probably isn't going to make much of a difference."

I refused to believe that. "Maybe not on my own, but if I had help? If I had you and Grandmother…"

"I think it's best we leave it to Etty," Mrs Sanders continued, moderation calming her tones. "I'm sure she'll find Emilie soon."

"How?" My voice sounded small and desperate. "I'm the only one who knows where she is."

"Well, if Etty comes back and hasn't found her, then you can tell her. Throwing yourself back into danger isn't going to help the situation at all."

"But by then it might be too late."

"Alphie dear, there isn't a 'too late'. It's not as if her parents are going to kill her."

"That's not what I meant."

"I know, but it's best that we wait for Etty. You'll stay here tonight."

It was a kind command, but a command nonetheless and it frustrated me. The twins and I plodded up the stairs to Zander's room. He shared it with Fabian, but thankfully Fabian had remained downstairs with the adults.

"She said she wanted to stay?" Zander's tone was a horror-stricken mixture of incredulity and concern. "I mean, I get that they're her parents and all, but seriously? We've all heard stories about what happened in the Resurgence of Evil. Your parents ..." He stopped suddenly, an apologetic expression lowering his face.

"We're all well-acquainted with such stories," I replied, sweeping over Zander's pause. "We actually visited a friend of my grandmother's, an elderly gentleman named Benny, the very afternoon we were kidnapped. He told us some horrific stories about Jonas and Myra."

"We know Benny," Lori whispered. "Mother often goes and visits him and Azariah – his carer. Benny and Azariah share a father."

So that was who Azariah was.

"I wish my grandmother was here." I sounded desolate. The twins nodded in agreement before falling silent.

"You know we can't just twiddle our thumbs and wait for her. I know your mother seems to think that's best, but no-one knows how long she may be, and I'm petrified of what will happen to Emilie."

Lori pursed her lips pointedly, inciting me, urging me

to push on.

"You didn't see her," I said. "Even those few days changed her, and now that I'm not there to reason or argue with her, she's completely at the mercy of her parents."

"And now she probably thinks you've abandoned her," Zander added, looking uncharacteristically serious.

The truth cut. I hoped she'd trust me – I hoped she'd trust that I was doing the right thing, but I wasn't so sure anymore.

"I agree that we have to rescue her – the real question is how." I was relieved to hear the vigour in Lori's voice, it bolstered me.

"What about the caravan?" Zander suggested. "We could use it to get to the field and then transfer to another caravan and caravan hop to Dalehead – I think I have a friend who lives there so we can see if he's willing to let us use his caravan."

It was a thin hope, but I nodded as it was our best option. Or rather, our only option.

"That won't work."

"And why not, Lori?" Zander demanded.

"Mum would never let us set foot in the caravan now – I can guarantee that she will be watching it like a hawk. She knows we won't want to just sit quietly by."

"We have to at least try," her brother combated defiantly.

It was true. We exited the house under the pretext of

desiring fresh air, and sure enough Mrs Sanders followed and carefully locked the caravan, before re-entering the house to hawk-eye us from the kitchen window.

"I told you," Lori whispered, as we mulled around outside to pass off our lie. "There's no getting out that way."

"Could we steal the key tonight?" I asked.

"Nope, doubt it. We'll have to come up with something else."

We trudged back inside three hearts heavier and sat down in frustrated silence. It was at least ten minutes' worth of ponderings later that Lori exclaimed: "I have an idea!"

She jumped up and rushed upstairs, Zander and I following behind, bemused but intrigued. Lori made her way back into Zander's room. Fabian was perched on his bed.

"We need your help, Fabes," Lori entreated.

"Ahh, I thought it might come to that." he replied, slipping us a small smirk. He seemed pleased that we had come to him. "Tell me the plan then, Lori."

She sat down beside him and began.

***

Alphie

Dinner was a rather tumultuous affair, as it always is in

222

the Sanders household. I remembered back to the first time that Lori and Zander had invited me to their house for dinner, the day we had properly become chums. We were seven, before Visi or Ally were born, but even with two children fewer and less infantile wailing around, it was still a cacophonous, noisy venture. If only I was as care-free now as I had been on that day …

I tried to cheer up for Mrs Sanders' sake; I knew she was only doing what she thought to be best. I also tried not to dwell on how we were going to deliberately disobey her that night. She had always been the only one to offer me any true motherly comfort – Grandmother being far too forbidding to be greatly maternal – and so I was loathe to betray that trust and affection. But I had no choice.

Lori, Zander, and Fabian acted so naturally that I almost forgot what we were planning to do. *Almost.* We all helped tidy up after dinner before excusing ourselves early on the pretence of getting an early night. Mrs Sanders watched us until we had rounded the corner of the stairs. I imagined her still below, prowling to make sure we didn't try anything desperate.

Fabian had been moved in with Visi so that I could share Zander's room. He bore it admirably, especially for a seventeen-year-old forced to share with a five-year-old, but I supposed he knew that he wasn't going to while away the whole night there.

We had agreed on midnight. It seemed fittingly 'Emilie' when I had suggested it. I smiled at the thought of our adventure to the Rhisa that one night, and how scared I had been. That was nothing compared to this. I only hoped that my courage had grown alongside my powers.

I didn't mean to, but I slept like a certain princess Emilie may have mentioned to me a few thousand times, thoroughly exhausted from the strain of the day. Zander shook me awake, grinning at my sleep-heavy confusion. The digital clock on the table beside me read 11:56. We arose and got dressed before tiptoeing down the stairs, wincing at every creak. Lori was already there. Just Fabian to wait for now. My watch read midnight. I shifted on the spot, willing him to materialise. Which he thankfully did two minutes later, shuffling soundlessly as he took the car keys from the drawer by the door.

"Sorry, I thought Visi might have been restless and so had to wait. We're all good now."

We moved as one single silent body to the door.

"Fabes?" The questioning voice rang out with undeniable sweetness, but it made us all jump.

Fabian turned. "Shh, Visi, go back to bed." He used his most encouraging, adult-styled tones.

"Where are you going?"

"Nowhere, it's fine."

"You're going to find her aren't you? Mummy said you shouldn't. I'm going to get Mummy."

"No, Visi, please."

But he was gone.

"Quick," Fabian hissed. "Everyone into the car."

We ran to its shadowed form. Zander took the passenger's seat and Lori and I leapt into the back. Fabian pulled away as we clumsily buckled our seatbelts. Lori gave a hysterical laugh.

"Well, that was close!"

I nodded, buoyed by the thrill and the risk of being caught. The narrowness of our escape had made my heart beat to a modulation which spurred me on. I grinned. We were off to find Emilie.

CHAPTER EIGHTEEN

Alphie

J gave the instructions from the back. It was harder in the dark, but luckily Dalehead was well signposted. The closer we got, the more intently I scanned for the point where the path I had taken met the road. We made it all the way into Dalehead and I still hadn't glimpsed it. I cursed quietly – this was more of a challenge than I had anticipated, and only the first step in an overtly complex plan. Fabian patiently turned around to comb back along the road, the others quizzing me increasingly less patiently about precisely what it had looked like. After ten minutes of driving back in the other direction, I knew that we had once again gone too far. It was impossible to see the path in the coal-black night.

"You said that you followed a river?" asked Fabian. I nodded, not seeing how that helped, since I was without a clue as to how to get back to the river.

"Well why don't we go back to that bridge a mile back and follow the river from there – I'm assuming it must be the same one."

"Fabes, you are a genius!" Lori exclaimed.

"Only doing my bit." He winked at her, but I could tell he was glad to have been the one to think of it.

Fabian stayed with the car while the three of us combed the riverbank, hugging it as closely as we dared in the stumbling darkness. Eventually we traced our way back to where the river had spat me out, then to where it had swallowed me up, and finally to a thankfully recognisable copse of trees. We could feel the time of the night wearing on.

It was Lori who spotted it first – a small collection of star-bright windows, shrouded in the monstrous silhouette of a manor house, just a sloped field away from us. I pointed out the iron-shielded gate I had slipped under earlier that day.

Once our success had been sufficiently but inaudibly celebrated, Zander reminded us that the walk from the car had taken at least thirty minutes. Too far for a getaway run, Lori wisely pointed out. It was frustrating standing in the trees just within the call of the gate. I wanted to rush in and sweep Emilie out of there and far away, but I knew planning is key to the success of any mission.

And so, we headed back towards the car, turning away from the house and following the track to where we hoped it would meet the road. It did – just past the village. We walked through the sleepy houses, trying to keep as quiet as possible. We reckoned three youngsters wandering around at one o'clock in the morning might look a little suspicious. The trek back along the road felt like an eternity, but in reality, it couldn't have been more than a couple of miles. We met no cars. At one point a fox ran across the road, causing Lori to scream and Zander to immediately fling his hand over her mouth.

"Shhh! You sound like a blinking car alarm!" he whispered, half-joking, half-severe. I doubted there was anyone around to detect the sound, but its pitchy squeal still jumped our hearts into our throats.

Fabian was standing outside of the car; the burdensome, weighted look on his face vanished when he saw us.

"I was beginning to wonder how I'd break the news of your disappearance to Mum! You were gone for over an hour."

Zander looked at his watch sheepishly. "Sorry, but good news – we found where Emilie's being kept."

We all climbed back into the car and set off, purring through the village. Zander pointed to the track, mimicking the exaggerated focus of a sniffer-dog, and we crawled up it with as much stealth as the vehicle could muster, headlights off and engine low, right until the house crept into sight. Fabian then switched into reverse and trundled off the track until the car was just out of the manor's eyeline.

"I want Lori to stay with the car." We now stood, gearing up to go.

"What? No way!"

"You stay here – Zander, Alphie, and I will get to the manor. I'll distract the guards as planned. You two will go find Emilie. You practised what to say to her, right? Remember, if I don't come back, Zander, you'll have to attempt to drive. If you're stopped, show them my licence and pretend to be me."

The plan sounded official in his deepened teenaged tones, empty of doubtful pauses.

"Woah, hold up, isn't that a bit extreme?" Zander said, haltingly taking the licence.

"Who knows. It's the only plan I have. As long as there aren't any more defences than Alphie says there are, I should be able to get back and drive you all home."

I felt guilty for sounding so certain about the manor's defences. In reality I only knew about what I'd already seen – the guards and the dogs. But my thoughts were interrupted by a persistent Lori.

"I am not staying here!" she repeated, attempting to sound matter of fact instead of petulantly childlike.

"Yes, you are – we don't need a rescue mission of four. Your job is the most important, if someone comes and takes the car, there's no getting away."

"Just because I'm the girl. If it's so important why don't you do it."

"Fine." He knew there was no point arguing, she would either come with them or follow after. "Zander, you stay with the car."

"No way."

Fabian sighed and rolled his eyes. We were wasting time.

"Okay, we'll all go," he decided. "Come on."

We proceeded to the gates. They stood menacing, immovable.

"Well? Dig us in then Alphie!" Zander winked at me.

It was easier this time, the dirt had been replaced over my hole from earlier, but the earth was still loose. It took very little energy to uncover and widen the hole again. Fabian insisted on going first. He wriggled through fine, although it was a rather comical sight. But just as he raised his head, a bark resounded and two dogs came charging towards him, teeth gnashing, eyes hunting. The guards must have let them loose to garrison the gate. I stood there, rooted to the spot, unable to tear my eyes away, the guilt of leading my friends' brother to his death suddenly overwhelming.

"Stop," Fabian said to the dogs, not in a plea or a shout but soothed in certainty and calm. He didn't seem afraid at all. And to my utter astonishment, stop they did. Of course, Fabian could talk to animals. But that didn't guarantee they would obey him, although many animals did, drawn by the bond. Now they were swaddled around him, licking his face and whimpering quietly. I laughed under my breath and crawled through after him. There was no movement, no men had hurried out to stop us, and so I forced myself to assume that they

230

hadn't heeded the bark.

The most hair-raising part was walking through the guard's living room again. It was deserted, the door still unlocked, but every step brought a sickening sensation to my throat. I guided the way across the room to the door which led to the corridor. Fabian brought up the rear and crouched behind the sofa closest to the exit, bundled over and prepared to guard our escape route. He rolled up his sleeves.

The corridor was exactly how I remembered it. The lamps were burning low in the early morning. In the dark, the odd bare lamp caused splodges to appear on the wooden panels, forming like dark ink stains in the corners. Ink stains, or blood? The thought made me gulp and I pushed it away, rehearsing over in my mind our plan. *In and out, don't be seen.*

I had to believe this would work. Desperation made me believe in Emilie, especially now that I had the twins with me. I knew that she would come with us.

She couldn't have liked it here by herself. When she saw we'd all come to rescue her she would leap up and we would run away together. *All of us.* Jonas and Myra would wake up and find her gone, they would never know what had happened and by the time they began to search for us we would be safely back at Grandmother's. Simple. I played it over and over in my mind. *Simple.*

We paused at the foot of the staircase, which I had figured out must be the way to the bedrooms – I assumed they would have relocated Emilie to a proper bedroom after I'd left. Zander took a seat hiding in the shadow of the stairwell, and crossed his arms in a show of bravery, as if to combat the quivering of his lip. I nodded to Lori, and we were about to start up the staircase when we heard a gentle moan in the distance. We stopped, stepped back into the corridor, looking around in panic for any trace of another person's presence.

Our breaths jolted in the tension of the air. We heard the moan for a second time.

"I think it's coming from down there," whispered Lori. She was pointing at the doorway to the cavern.

The moans grew in volume, the sound of someone so evidently in pain making us wince.

"Is that Emilie?" Zander whispered.

"What if she did something to upset her parents and they hurt her and threw her back in the cavern?" Lori added, her voice strained with concern.

It was a risk to check, but a risk we'd have to take. Someone, even if it wasn't Emilie, was clearly in pain. Zander waited on the stairs leading down to the cavern for us, assuming his role as a guard once more.

Lori and I approached the door to the cavern thankfully once again unlocked.

Together, Lori and I descended into the darkness. The light from the corridor spilled a couple of metres into the room but beyond that, only darkness. I felt Lori's fingers touch mine and I grabbed onto them, thankful for her presence. We walked deeper into the cavern. All the furniture seemed to have been removed, making it more like a prison. Every inch of me shuddered as I walked once again into my confinement, whispering Emilie's name and hearing it resonate eerily off the walls. The skylight cast a greyish ball of moonlight into the cell, and in that we could just make out a hunched figure lying on some straw.

Emilie.

***

Emilie

I tossed about in my bed. I couldn't sleep. My parents had tried to cheer me up by telling me that I didn't need him. That my life was better without him and that now I needed only them.

But they were wrong. I didn't need them either.

The only person I can trust is myself. I repeated it again and again.

But the truth was that here, in this manor house, I was more powerful. Here was where I would do best, alongside them. I needed them as trainers if not as parents.

After I had fainted in the weather Rhisa and been plunged into darkness for the second time, my parents decided that I'd done enough training for the day. Instead, they gave me a tour of the place, enjoying showing off every corridor, room, and even the cavern, as if proud creators of some magnificent design. I didn't care that much for their attitude and didn't try to pretend, and they ended up leaving me in a new room. I had collapsed gratefully onto the bed, ignoring the burst of dust which it produced and instead focussing on the softness of the mattress. I had willed myself desperately to sleep. Sleep would free me from the numbness that had overcome me in the Rhisa and only grown with Alphie's desertion.

I had even tried crying to get myself to sleep. I'd often tired myself out through crying. It normally makes whatever torment I'm experiencing a lot easier to handle – more romantic, more comforting. But as I tried to force tears, I found that I couldn't. Instead, I came across an emptied lake – just as I had when I'd tried to force moisture from the cloud that afternoon. I relented, letting the darkness of night enter the room and grow around me, filling me. Caring hurt too much. Questions hurt too much. Much better to just give in to the emptiness. The only person who properly cared about me was me.

***

"Well well well. What have we here?"

A man's voice - the guard's voice. It was a trap; we'd been led into a trap. I heard Lori's sharp intake of breath, felt her grip on my hand tighten, or maybe I tightened my grip on hers.

The man chuckled quietly and rose, towering towards us.

"Run Zander!" Lori exploded from beside me. She had thought only of her twin in her moment of panic.

"Now, now, little missy, that's not going to do anything."

We turned as if to race back, but the guard was on us and binding us with ropes he had been carrying and leading us out of the cavern. We hadn't even had a chance to try anything, so swift was his move.

Zander was in the corridor, looking like a rabbit caught in headlights – but one that knew he was about to be run over. Why hadn't he run to Fabian?

It wasn't long before it became apparent why. The other guard had Fabian tied up just as we were, blocking the exit back the way we had come. None of us had realised that fear would debilitate our powers so much, rendering them useless. I willed Zander to run – somewhere, anywhere. And run he did, down the corridor and into the door which Emilie had said led to the hall.

Harry laughed in a pitiless bark, holding tight to both Lori and me, and inclined his head. "Shall we follow?" he sneered.

CHAPTER NINETEEN

Alphie

J was struck by the grandiose sweep of the hall, even after Emilie's description. It really did look like it had no ceiling. Zander was in the centre of the room, standing frozen in shock, staring at the far end of the space, where three chairs were placed on a dais. It was easy for the other guard to tie him up too.

We were led across the room. It would have been useless to run – we'd have fallen over with our hands tied behind our back. But running wasn't the thought that most occupied our minds, because sitting on the middle chair, placed purposefully between her smug parents, arms resting languidly by her side, was the very person we had sought. Her eyes gazed at us passively, almost carelessly, in a way that panicked me, more so than anything else I had endured over the past couple of days. Emilie showed no flicker of emotion – even hatred would have been better than the cool indifference she now fixed me with. What had happened?

"Welcome back, Alphie," boomed Jonas. His voice was deep, but not in a rich way, in a way that made you think of the bottom of a ravine where all number of creatures had fallen to their death.

"Did you really think we wouldn't have any other defences than the dogs? I guess you never realised that Bill has the gift of sight. It works… differently, more effectively, than Etty's pathetic guardians." He smirked. "We've been expecting you. And expecting your empathy to cripple you."

I squirmed in my bonds as Jonas continued. "And now you've brought your little friends with you too. How kind. Why do you think we let you escape the first-time round?"

Let me escape? But what of the guards' conversation about keeping a close eye on me, what about the chase of the dogs – had it all been an act?

Jonas sugared us with a smile. "We've got the most wonderful plans for you all."

"Not if we can stop you!" yelled Lori, before being pushed to her knees by Bill with a grunt. I was surprised by her passion and her courage to speak. I had only silence.

"Oh, do calm down, dear," smiled Myra. "There's no need to be so rude – I don't even think we've had a proper introduction, although I'm sure Alphie told you lots about us." She turned back to me. "We knew your parents, Alphie dear, they were good people. Too good. That was their undoing. Just like yours really." Her tones still sparkled.

I gritted my teeth as rage frothed inside, a heat unfamiliar to me. She had killed them. I knew it from the sickly grin plastered on her smiling face. It was her and Jonas who had killed them.

"Of course, their deaths were really Etty's fault," she continued. "Etty's fault for trying to banish us from the family. From trying to hide our true powers, our true potential."

I looked to Emilie, hoping for a flash of remorse, outrage, anything, but her eyes remained reticent, empty.

"Emilie, we've come to rescue you." Lori's voice rang out sweet and clear, well-rehearsed in her head.

"Rescue her?" Jonas laughed, "From what? Her parents, her family? I think you'll find she's perfectly fine here."

"Don't listen to him, Emilie, *we're* your family." Lori pleaded with her. It was the speech we had practised in the car. Emilie's eyes raised up slightly. Was there a flicker of doubt in her eyes? It was gone as soon as it came but the flash gave me hope.

"What would your *real* parents say, Emilie?" I added, encouraged.

"Real parents?!" Myra mimicked. "We are her real parents. Who gave birth to her? Whose blood is the blood that flows through her?"

"It's true," Emilie responded. Her voice sounded distant, far away.

"No, it's not." My voice was frantic as I continued, "A family is more than just blood; it's love, it's kindness, it's care."

"Is that why you abandoned me then?" Her eyes fixed on me now, boring into me, trying to crush me with the weight of her anger and hurt. *I had hurt her.*

"No. I thought you trusted me. I left so I could find help and come back for you. And I did come back – look, I'm here now." I felt cowed and thought I sounded it too.

The man sniggered. "Don't listen to him, Emilie. He came back to get information, to sneak around. We caught him upstairs trying to explore our Rhisa." The lies burnt. "He just wants to use you, Emilie, to gain information for his own ends," Jonas finished, a hint of triumph wavering his tone.

"No!" The words tumbled out of me with a new desperation. "That's what they're doing. They're poisoning you against Etty, using you to get to her, that's why they suddenly want to be your parents again. They're experimenting on you with stolen powers. That's why-"

"Enough," Jonas exploded. "Take them away." He turned to his wife while an ugly grin, smothered in ambition, warped his features. "Soon we'll have some lovely new Rhisa from their powers, my dear."

"Emilie!" Lori screamed, echoed by Zander. I could hear them straining at their bonds, but the second that either of them used their telekinesis to loosen the ropes, Harry tightened them all the more fiercely. Of course, his powers were stronger. He was an adult, and fully trained.

But then, just as we were about to be dragged out of the door, I saw the spark of an idea light up Zander's eyes.

"Lori, the chairs!" he screamed.

I turned, and as I did, I watched as the chairs were swept out from under Emilie's parents' feet. It was a genius idea by Zander, the perfect use of combined telekinesis. And it truly was a confounding spectacle – had it been different circumstances I might have even laughed. Harry and Bill were temporarily stunned, unsure of what to do, and as Jonas and Myra rose, trying to regain composure, Fabian leapt from his bonds, letting them fall to the floor.

Whilst we had been trying to reason, he must have been focussing on undoing his ropes. But by hand, not with his powers – a simplicity no-one had expected. The two guards lurched towards him, dropping all our bonds and their grip of Zander, but they were stopped midway by his fallen ropes, which had bounded up from their lifeless slumber to encircle the guards in the air, whipping their faces and enclosing around them. I turned to see Lori controlling the ropes, even with her hands still tied.

"Zander!" I cried. "Untie us!"

Soon all our bonds had fallen to the floor. I shook my wrists in relieved freedom. I looked around for Jonas and Myra, but they were nowhere to be seen. Zander started to help Lori keep the guards in check, but even through the pain of the whip strokes, Bill and Harry were beginning to fight back.

"Go to her!" cried Fabian from across the room.

Ignoring the struggle around me, I turned and cannonballed towards the dais, intent on making Emilie listen to me. I grabbed her with both hands and held onto her, keeping her at arm's length so that I could look into her eyes. Fabian stood behind me as protection, hopefully keeping an eye out for Jonas and Myra.

"Emilie! Emilie, look at me. Listen to me." I lifted her chin so that she had no choice but to look in my eyes. "A family isn't joined by blood, it's joined by love, and that bond is stronger than any other. Your parents, who raised you, love you; your sister loves you; Etty loves you and we love you. If we didn't why would we come back for you?" I could see pain in the blue and green specks of her eyes, the desperation, and the beginning of tears.

I was desperate too. The speech had sounded better in the car.

"You've got to make a choice, Emilie, and it's a choice only you can make. Yes, these people are your biological parents, and yes, the blood that flows in you flows also in them. But that isn't what defines you. Your choices are what define you. And that choice now is who you decide to trust."

"I only trust myself." The words were meant to be certain, but they came out sounding like those of an insecure and petulant child. I could tell she heard it too.

"I'm sorry to hear that," I said, ducking to avoid a chair leg that Zander and Lori were moving to fend off an attack. "I had hoped you trusted me."

I stepped away again. Mrs Sanders had been right. This was a bad idea, we alone couldn't do it, we couldn't bring Emilie back. I felt the weight of the situation bearing down on me. I had got us into this situation, my stupidity had led us into the trap, and I hadn't been enough to change Emilie's mind. I stepped backwards from the dais, the thought of failure consuming me, making me see nothingness. See a void. A blank. Words left me.

But then I saw them: Jonas and Myra. They had slipped behind the twins and were summoning a blockade of darkness that was growing like a wave about to obliterate the whole room. They hadn't cared what I said to Emilie. They had known I wasn't going to change her mind, just like they'd known I'd return. They had only been focussed on their power, on gathering their strength, on finding a place where they could assert their darkness over the whole room.

Lori, Zander, Fabian. Only metres away from the wall. The darkness, I could see tendrils reaching out towards them, fingertips of obsidian intent on seizing them. But the Sanders were not going to die on my account. *Not today.* The decision permeated through my whole being, filling me with a strength that I had never felt before. And then it happened.

CHAPTER TWENTY

Emilie

J didn't know what to think. I sat there passively, letting the words of my parents and the words of my friends wash over me. It had been easy.

I had been surprised when my parents had entered my room, saying that those I had once called my friends had broken in, trying to spy on us, trying to destroy the Rhisa. Alphie and Lori had said they were rescuing me. I didn't know who to trust, I didn't want to choose.

I can only trust myself. The words seemed so hollow, so empty. How had I come to this? I saw the look of hurt and disappointment, the look of resignation in Alphie's eyes as he stepped back away from me. I didn't want him to go. I also wasn't sure that I wanted to stay. But if I could only trust myself – where *was* I to go? My parents held the easier option. My parents held the key to power, power which would stop me from being reliant on anyone else. No rules, no barriers. I could do what I wanted and be who I wanted. But that wasn't much help if I didn't know what it was that I wanted.

Alphie's eyes turned to determination as he stepped off the dais. Lori and Zander had managed to knock out one of the guards with chair legs. The strength of their powers surprised me, and evidently surprised the guard as well. Fabian was in hand-to-hand combat with Bill, whose power of sight wasn't any help to him now, engaged in a battle of fists and kicks. And the wall of darkness crept ever closer to them. I could tell that they couldn't win, that much was obvious. I vaguely wondered what would happen when the darkness reached them. I wasn't sure I wanted to find out, but it didn't look like I'd have much choice in the matter.

And then it happened.

Out of Alphie's hands, as if from inside him, came a plume of fire.

It plunged through the room, separating the twins from the guards, its sparks feeding off the chairs which they hurriedly released, gaining strength, gaining power. It was alive.

Alphie had done it. He had truly done it. He had produced fire. And all of a sudden, I wanted to clap and cheer as I had on Etty's front lawn. As he had for me. Memories flooded through me, his craziness, his charm, his care. The way he had been scared of exploring the house at night but had somehow found the courage to come back here. And suddenly I knew he hadn't come back to snoop; he'd come back to rescue me. It was as if his fire had burned a hole through the confusion of my troubled mind. As if his fire had purified my thoughts and refined them as only fire can. I felt its heat, saw its brilliant light. I felt clarity pulsing through me. I felt light and giddy.

Alphie was good. That much I was certain of.

A tight ball of emotions hit me hard, right in the stomach. I knew what I wanted. I wanted Alphie to hold me and let me cry as he had that last night in the cell, to tell me it was all going to be alright. But it wasn't, was it? It was most definitely not alright.

Alphie had said I had a choice. I wasn't helpless in my numbness. I knew in that instant that I would choose Alphie and my friends. Always, over and over, no matter how many times I was asked to, no matter how many times they let me down.

"Alphie!" I screamed with my whole being.

***

Alphie

She screamed my name. And I faltered. She was on the other side of the fire, the fire that I had somehow been able to produce. The guards were stunned, seated, defenceless. We were heading for the corridor, heading for freedom. And then a burst of light ripped through my flames, leaving a temporary opening, and Emilie hurtled through, laughing and unscathed. I stared in amazement.

And then I felt a push against my fire. The darkness from behind. Emilie's parents. The tendrils of darkness pushed back against my flames from one side. Then from the other side too. Their power was strong. They must have spent decades perfecting it, growing it in ways I couldn't even begin to fathom. My fire couldn't survive against the growing darkness. It even invaded my head, filling my mind with a blackness that swooped around the edges of my brain. A tomb. A wretched feeling of despair.

But then Emilie was beside me, hands outstretched, adding light to my weakening fire. And her light was blinding; I was stunned, spell-bound, stupefied. Our firelight grew, until it too was like a wall. The darkness pushed back against us, but our wall held firm. It shook and wobbled in places, but I dug deep and kept pushing. I felt Emilie doing the same beside me. We thrust our arms forwards and screamed, screaming out our power to help it heave back the assailing darkness.

I didn't even know that it was possible to combine our powers. But it was working. I turned and saw the other three Sanders stumbling out of the hall and down the corridor, shock and awe mirrored on their face.

Then we turned, leaving the firelight-wall blazing behind, and ran. Emilie reached for my hand and squeezed it. The squeeze said a million difficult words and I accepted them. We dashed into the corridor. Now that our powers were no longer feeding the fire, I knew it wouldn't be long before Jonas and Myra followed. Zander was just squeezing out of the hole, with Fabian and Lori already on the other side. Fabian had positioned the dogs in a protective semi-circle around the gate. We dashed past them and they paid us no heed. I shoved Emilie down and she scrambled through the gap and then I swiftly followed. I could hear the dogs barking behind me, a tell-tale sign that the guards had come out. But I was on the other side of the gate, and we were legging it down the drive back to the car, back to safety.

***

Emilie

I ran alongside them, laughing. It's funny how once you make a choice, once you make up your mind, everything feels better. Alphie was right. It's your choices that define you, and I had made mine. I had made many since I had been sent to Aunt Etty's, some of them not so great, but every one had shaped me. I knew that I'd be faced with many more choices ahead of me, but for now I basked in the joy of this one.

They had a car waiting down the drive – I guess that's why they'd brought Fabian. The sun hadn't yet risen but the sky was full of the dawn, tinged yellow around the edges. I could hear a bird, somewhere up ahead, welcoming in the new day. Its music filled me, and it was joined by more birdsong until I understood why people called it a dawn chorus. I wanted to join in too.

We clambered into the car. Alphie even gave me a rapid flourish of "Ladies first," as I entered, his old self restored. I ended up squished in the back, with Alphie in between me and Lori. I could feel the warmth of his leg against mine and all of a sudden I was swamped by exhaustion. I rested my head on Alphie's shoulder and watched the sun rise across the country roads, washing the fields clean in golden light and chasing the trees who seemed reluctant for their morning bath of amber. I too felt washed clean from the confusion and despair of the past few days, by the light Alphie and I had produced. A deep gratitude welled up inside me – for the warmth of the car, for my friends, for whoever had made such a glorious sunrise.

The rolling of the car lulled me, and I closed my eyes. There would be consequences for my wrong actions, but I knew that I would learn and grow through them. Wasn't that what mistakes were for after all?

My parents had tried to use me, tried to experiment on me, tried to steal my friends' powers. But we had escaped. Myself twice over – in the flesh and in the mind. I hoped I was stronger than their lies.

I was vaguely aware of the car stopping, of strong arms wrapping around me and helping me out. Of soft pillows and hushed voices, a chink of light through drawn curtains and the distant crash of waves.

**

Azariah

The moment I saw her I almost cried. Etty's elation had turned the sky sapphire. Trust Jonas and Myra to outwit us by choosing a location so close to home, hidden from view within our own concentration of Potensa power. And I saw her in front of me. She was flesh and blood, not light and shadows of the mind. I had given up on trying to reach her with my powers, I had been on the brink of giving in completely – you could probably tell from how silent I've been. And then there she was, crumpled up in the backseat of a car, head dozing on Alphie's shoulder.

Etty and I had arrived back early that morning, more despondent than ever. But as we stepped out from the Darwala, we were stopped by a tearful Mrs Sanders, her mournful skirts wailing outwards in the wind. She was breathless and panicked, and her story came in short, sharp bursts of desperation. Alphie's return, her children's disobedience, the missing car – the tumult of the night spurted from her cracked lips. We took her home for a cup of tea, Etty and I silent and separated from her maternal fear, each of us attempting to form a plan in our heads. But as we approached her front door, as the morning's light began to grow, we saw the unexpected sitting in her driveway.

"The car!" cried Mrs Sanders from behind her tears, pulling away from us to hurl herself towards it.

And that's when we saw the children.

Lori, Zander, Alphie and Fabian attempted between broken whispers to explain the story without waking the sleeping Emilie. Our looks of astonishment grew wider as they continued and by the end, I couldn't help but be impressed. I noted concern in Etty at the mention of the other Rhisa, but I pushed it aside – this moment was for celebration. Fabian and the twins were ushered inside by their mother, whilst Mr Sanders offered to drive the rest of us back up the hill. Alphie too fell asleep on the drive.

Mr Sanders, Etty, and I carried the children out of the car and inside the manor. But at the tapestry protecting the tower, Etty paused, explaining that she hadn't been inside since she was forced to banish Jonas and Myra. Etty had never quite gotten over the pain of her niece and nephew's desertion and it struck me as strange that she had put Emilie in Myra's old room. But who was I to question her decision?

I was, however, shocked to be met with their portrait on entering Emilie's bedroom. I took it down carefully once Emilie was safely in bed and brought it out to Etty who surveyed it grimly.

"I'd forgotten it was still in there," was her only explanation. "Probably about time we got rid of it."

I half nodded, now was not the time for questions,

and together with Mr Sanders we headed downstairs,
minds and hearts still reeling from the events and news
of the past few days.

CHAPTER TWENTY-ONE

Emilie

I awoke with a start, remembering the events of the night. The curtains were mostly drawn, but a soft beam of light floated through the channel where they met. I was back in my room at Aunt Etty's. I looked to the wall across from me, dreading the eyes that would meet me, but they were no longer there. Someone must have taken the massive portrait down as I slept. In its place was a small, framed watercolour of the sea, gentle waves lapping across the streaks of sand. I realised that Alphie still hadn't taken me to the beach yet. I would have to make him take me tomorrow. I lay back and sighed. I was still tired, in that almost sticky state of having finally slept after a long period of time, but I was awake now, and there was plenty to do and say.

I got up, shoving my feet into the sky-blue slippers,

and stepped into the hallway. There was no answer to my knock at Alphie's door – he must have already gone downstairs. I didn't really want to go down and face Aunt Etty. I felt guilty for doubting her, but I also couldn't quite shake the feeling of mistrust that Jonas and Myra had seeded in me.

But I knew that it couldn't be avoided forever. I'd even have to tell my adopted parents – my true parents – about my whole escapade. And I'd have to tell Lizzie about everything too – I knew that now. She was wrong about magic, but so right about trusting in logic and family, in what you know to be true.

I made my way downstairs, pacing the now-familiar path to the kitchen. I could smell something delightful and my stomach rose in answer. I turned left into the low-roofed kitchen and there they all were. Alphie, Etty, Lori, Zander, Fabian, and Mrs Sanders. Even Benny's caregiver was there, which surprised me somewhat.

I stood rather sheepishly in the door – Alphie would have told them everything and I felt embarrassed by my mistrust and by the way I had been beguiled and tricked by Jonas and Myra. By the way that I had looked inwards for the faith that they had always provided me with. Aunt Etty rose. I hung my head. But then all of a sudden, I could feel arms around me, and I found myself in her strong embrace.

"I'm so, so sorry," I was saying, muffled by her shawl and my tears.

"No, I should have been more honest with you." She

pulled away and smiled gently, wiping the tears from my face. I'd never seen the lines of her face so soft before.

"You must be starving," Alphie said from across the table. A bubble of laughter escaped me despite it all, and I nodded.

I sat and ate, knowing that I would have to offer up more apologies, and far more explanations afterwards, but also secure in the knowledge that I would be forgiven. Because that's what love does. And it hurt. But it was so much better than empty darkness.

***

Azariah

In that moment as I watched her from across the table, enjoying the bittersweet, joyful reunion, I felt relief loosen all my fears from the last few days. Much work still had to be done, but for the time being I was content to ignore it, to sit in cosy reconciliation. I knew the road ahead for Emilie was not straight or easy, it had many twists and turns. But I knew too that she had grown, that she was strong enough to face them. She was powerful. More importantly, she was good. And along the way she would have many to help her, to watch over her, to guide her, myself included – even if she didn't know it quite yet.

I told you, you'd come to care for her. Didn't I?

ALPHIE-ISMS

Abominably – (adverb) terribly, horribly

Abscond – (verb) to leave hurriedly

Absolve – (verb) to remove blame

Absurdities – (noun) peculiarities, strange things

Acquiesced – (verb) gave in, obeyed

Apathetic – (adj) uncaring

Apprehended – (verb) stopped

Ascended – (verb) climbed up

Assert – (verb) to make clear

Assertions – (noun) confirmations

Astringent – (adj) forbidding, cold

Audible – (adj) can be heard

Bedeck – (verb) decorate

Befuddled – (adj) confused

Bemused – (verb) confused

Blazoned – (verb) displayed proudly

Broaching – (verb) raising, introducing

Cacophonous – (adj) loud

Categorically – (adverb) absolutely

Chums – (noun) friends

Cloddish – (adj) foolish, clumsy

Compassionate – (adj) kind, caring

Confounding – (adj) surprising

Consigned – *(verb) left to*

Consoled – *(verb) comforted*

Consternation – *(noun) concern, upset*

Contemplate – *(verb) consider, think over*

Culmination – *(noun) end*

Cultivate – *(verb) grow, encourage*

Dais – *(noun) platform*

Debilitate – *(verb) to make weak*

Delectable – *(adj) delicious, attractive*

Demeanour – *(noun) manner*

Demise – *(noun) death*

Depleted – *(verb) empty, diminished*

Desolate – *(adj) distraught, having given up*

Detect – *(verb) pick up on*

Eloquent – *(adj) well-spoken*

Embrace – *(verb) welcome, hug*

Endeavour – *(verb) attempt*

Enkindle – *(verb) to set alight*

Estranged – *(adj) distant, unconnected*

Eternal – *(adj) forever*

Fathom – *(verb) to understand*

Flaunting – *(verb) showing off*

Flavoursome – *(adj) delicious*

Foolhardy – *(adj) bold, risky*

Forsaken – *(verb) left to, abandoned*

Fortitude – *(noun) strength*

Fortuitously – *(adverb) luckily*

Fractured – *(verb) broken, splintered*

Gentility – *(adj) kindness, politeness*

Grandiose – *(adj) impressive, grand*

Hastened – *(verb) hurried*

Hearsay – *(noun) someone else's speech, rumour*

Impugned – *(verb) challenged*

Incarcerated – *(verb) imprisoned*

Inclining – *(verb) leaning towards*

Indubitably – *(adverb) undoubtedly*

Ineffably – *(adj) a great amount*

Infantile – *(adj) childlike*

Insights – *(noun) inner information*

Interminable – *(adj) - eternal*

Intermittent – *(adj) not steady or continuous*

Languidly – *(adverb) loosely, lifelessly*

Loathe – *(verb) hate*

Magnanimously – *(adverb) generously, forgiving*

Malevolent – *(adj) evil*

Materialise – *(verb) appear*

Mementos – *(noun) little keepsakes, memories*

Misadventure – *(noun) accident*

Modulation – *(noun) change*

Morphed – *(verb) changed, transformed*

Negligible – *(adj) easily forgotten*

Nonchalantly – *(adverb) causally*

Oblivion – *(noun) to being forgotten*

Occasioned – *(verb) to come across*

Perceived – *(verb) noticed*

Perish – *(verb) die, suffer*

Perplexing – *(verb) confusing*

Perturbed – *(adj) anxious, unsettled*

Placidly – *(adverb) calmly*

Pliable – *(adj) easy to mould*

Pondered – *(verb) think carefully on*

Premises – *(noun) property*

Prestigious – *(adj) well respected*

Pretext – *(noun) reason, excuse*

Prolonged – *(verb) made longer than necessary*

Propellant – *(noun) something that pushes you*

Prospect – *(noun) plan*

Rampant – *(adj) wild*

Ravenous – *(adj) hungry, starving*

Rendezvous – *(noun) meet*

Resonate – *(verb) fill with a noise*

Sepulchral – (adj) gloomy

Shrouded – (verb) covered

Smothered – (verb) to cover and stop

Solitary – (adj) alone

Strident – (adj) loud and harsh

Striven – (verb) to make efforts towards

Succumbed – (verb) gave in

Sustenance – (noun) food, nourishment

Swaddled – (verb) bundled up

Swathed – (verb) bundled, wrapped

Tenacity – (noun) determination, strength

Transmitted – (verb) passed along

Trove – (noun) secret store

Tumultuous – (adj) loud and confused noise

Unambiguous – (adj) clear

Uncouth – (adj) rough, rude

Unequivocally – (adverb) unmistakeably

Ungraciously – (adverb) rudely

Unregal – (adj) not kingly or fine

Unscathed – (adj) unharmed

Unscripted – (verb) made up on the spot

Utterances – (noun) murmurs

Vamoose – (verb) to disappear

Vehemently *– (adverb)*
strongly

Veritably *– (adverb) truly*

Vitality *– (noun) strength*

Warped *– (verb)*
distorted, changed

Weedy *– (adj) weak*

Acknowledgements

To David, Thomas, Tabitha and Andrew - my incredible siblings whose imaginations helped inspire this novel. (And Alisha and Lauren, you may not remember it but one of the games we made up all together sparked the beginnings.)

To Thomas, because he said I had to acknowledge the fact that he suggested the title.

To my dad whose imaginary bedtime stories taught me to tell my own stories, and to my mum who taught me to read and write, and later taught me to deal with the difficult emotions that come with being a teenager.

To Emily Williams, for almost twenty years of friendship and for continually showing me that friendships are worth fighting for (and for inspiring our protagonist's name - don't tell Alex!).

I love you all and couldn't have done this without your encouragement, first reads, and perfectionism (yes that's you, Dad).

And obviously to Alex, who took pity on that little girl who didn't know anyone on the first day of school and asked to be her friend. You have changed my life.

Above all thank you to God, my Father, Lord and Saviour who has given me any gifts or skills I possess, may my part in this book be to your glory.

***

I dedicate this novel to each and every stapled scrap of papers I called a book when I was five. I dedicate this novel to the parents who lovingly admired each one, to the father whose intellect I inherited and the mother whose work ethic guided me. To my brothers who gave me the need for the escapism of a novel, but who also kept me young and imaginative. I dedicate this book to Nana Gigi, who showed me that life can be fun if you're only bold enough to dance on tables. And to Nana and Baba, who inspired my belief that romance is not confined to the words of a novel, that adventure can be found beyond the realms of fiction, and that life is worth fighting for when you believe in a cause. And finally, I would like to thank Phoebe, who, despite changing the characters' names a million times over to suit her "vision", has been the best writing partner, and more importantly, the best friend that a girl could ask for.

***

Thanks also to our wonderful team at Cranthorpe Millner. To Kirsty, for her patience in taking us through every stage from draft to page. To Sian, again for her patience through many cover drafts. To Shannon, for all her tips for publicity and her organisation. These people are the reason you hold this book in your hands.

About the authors

Phoebe and Alexandra have been best friends since the age of eleven. In Year 8, they started writing the novel that they themselves had always longed to read. Six years and many hours later, they finished their debut novel and started at Durham University together in September 2020. Studying English and History respectively as BA (Hons), both of them write for online magazines and frequently dabble in a bit of light poetry. Writing has brought the duo even closer together, sharing the innermost secrets of their imaginations and pouring their hearts and souls into their shared endeavour.